W9-DIW-875

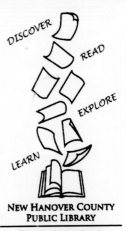

DISCOVER
READ
EXPLORE
LEARN

NEW HANOVER COUNTY
PUBLIC LIBRARY

If found, please return to:
201 Chestnut St.
Wilmington, NC 28401
(910) 798-6300
http://www.nhclibrary.org

John Lincoln Clem

Civil War Drummer Boy

Discard
NHCPL

SGT. JOHNNY CLEM

BASED *ON A* TRUE STORY

JOHN LINCOLN CLEM

CIVIL WAR
DRUMMER BOY

NEW HANOVER COUNTY
PUBLIC LIBRARY
201 CHESTNUT STREET
WILMINGTON. NC 28401

BY KRISTIN O'DONNELL TUBB WRITING AS

❊ E. F. ABBOTT ❊

WITH ILLUSTRATIONS BY STEVEN NOBLE

FEIWEL AND FRIENDS NEW YORK

A Feiwel and Friends Book
An Imprint of Macmillan

John Lincoln Clem: Civil War Drummer Boy.
Text copyright © 2016 by Macmillan. Illustrations copyright © 2016 by Steven Noble.
All rights reserved.

Printed in the United States of America by R. R. Donnelley & Sons Company,
Harrisonburg, Virginia. For information, address Feiwel and Friends,
175 Fifth Avenue, New York, N.Y. 10010.

Our books may be purchased in bulk for promotional, educational, or business use.
Please contact your local bookseller or the Macmillan Corporate and Premium
Sales Department at (800) 221-7945 ext. 5442 or by e-mail at
MacmillanSpecialMarkets@macmillan.com.

Library of Congress Cataloging-in-Publication Data

Abbott, E. F., author.
John Lincoln Clem : Civil War drummer boy / E. F. Abbott. — First edition.
pages cm. — (Based on a true story)
Summary: A fictional retelling of the legend of John Clem, who ran away from his
Ohio home to become a drummer boy during the Civil War, and became famous when he
was captured in 1863 and was exchanged after a short stay in Andersonville prison.
ISBN 978-1-250-06837-8 (hardcover) — ISBN 978-1-250-08030-1 (e-book)
1. Clem, John Lincoln, 1851–1937—Juvenile fiction.   2. Soldiers—United States—
Juvenile fiction.   3. United States—History—Civil War, 1861–1865—Juvenile fiction.
[1. Clem, John Lincoln, 1851–1937—Fiction.   2. Soldiers—Fiction.   3. United States—
History—Civil War, 1861–1865—Fiction.]   I. Title.
PZ7.1.A16Jo 2016   813.6—dc23   [Fic]   2015004151

Frontispiece: LC-DIG-ppmsca-34511

Book design by Anna Booth & April Ward
Feiwel and Friends logo designed by Filomena Tuosto

First Edition: 2016

1   3   5   7   9   10   8   6   4   2

mackids.com

BASED ON A TRUE STORY BOOKS

are exciting historical fiction about real children who lived through extraordinary times in American history.

———◦◦◦◦———

DON'T MISS:

Mary Jemison: Native American Captive

Nettie and Nellie Crook: Orphan Train Sisters

Sybil Ludington: Revolutionary War Rider

"I was the youngest soldier that served in the Civil War. Almost literally it might be said that I went from the nursery to the battlefield."

—Colonel John L. Clem,
The Outlook, July 4, 1914

The huge iron train wheels rumbled by, sounding to Johnny like a herd of wild mustangs, like thunder. Louder, even. Wind and dust stirred up under them. He felt small—bug-tiny—next to those things. Things that big and powerful and loud made it hard to be a hero. Johnny spat at them.

Johnny hated train wheels. And he hated feeling small and powerless.

He used to stand there, next to the dusty roar, and scream cuss words at those wheels. Then for a while he'd just scream. But it didn't make him feel any better, no, sir.

"Staring at them isn't going to bring her back, John Joseph," Pop said.

Johnny hadn't realized Pop had walked up. He shrugged. Did Pop think he didn't know that? He was nine, after all. He knew Mama wasn't coming back.

"Heard word that the troops are mustering in town this afternoon," Pop said.

"Really? Today's the day?" It was the one thing that could turn Johnny's sour mood sweet: Union troops! "Let's go!"

Pop smiled, patted Johnny's head (which made him feel like a kid), and walked back down the dusty road toward home. Johnny spat at the train wheels one more time, for good measure.

"I hate you."

<hr />

The town square in Newark, Ohio, was four dirt roads that cut across rocky ridges and miles of cornfields, and they all just happened to intersect at that spot. A handful of brick buildings stood squat along the square, and a small creek burbled nearby. Usually quiet. Usually boring.

But today! Today, the Union troops were mustering, and their gathering was quite the sight!

Today, the blasts of the mighty bugle could be heard from a half mile away.

Today, the smell of roasted chicken filled the air from the picnic baskets folks had packed for the troops.

Today, those usually boring brick buildings were decorated with red, white, and blue bunting. Ladies leaned out of second-story windows, throwing rose petals down on the crowd. Older women waved handkerchiefs (when they weren't honking their noses into them). Old men raised their canes and yelled "Hurrah!" and "Save the Union!" and "Beat back those fire-eaters!"

And the troops! There were so many of them— about a thousand men total. Gleaming brass buttons winked on knife-sharp blue uniforms. The soldiers held muskets and flags and musical instruments. Those men stood proud and tall. Those men stood like heroes.

It was, all of it, the most glorious sight Johnny had ever seen. His heart raced and his palms sweated and his chin lifted with Union pride.

A soldier with lots of colorful rope on his shoulders climbed atop a stump. Johnny had stood on that exact stump many times, cupping his hands around his mouth and shouting loud speeches about the high prices of sour apple candy sticks at the general store. But this guy! He didn't cup his hands or nothing.

Then a drum started beating, low and slow. Quiet at first, underneath the noise of crying mamas and guffawing men. The crowd almost didn't even notice it. Like a heartbeat, *taptaptap*.

But it grew louder, louder, swelling and rising with each beat until it was bouncing and echoing off the buildings, *BOOMBOOMBOOM*. People grew silent as the beat of the drum rumbled through their chests.

And when it stopped—when the drumbeat silenced—Johnny felt like someone had ripped his heart clean out. The whole crowd held its breath and waited to be told to exhale, because the drum had taken over. The drum did that.

For the first time ever, that drum made Johnny feel like he was a part of something big.

"Ladies and gentlemen!" the fancy fella on the stump said. He *said* things, he didn't *yell* them. That struck Johnny as important. He decided to weave through the crowd to get closer to this importance. Johnny bumped against the waists of adults wearing belt buckles and leather gun holsters and dress ribbons until he was just below the important fella.

"Ladies and gentlemen, the United States are no longer united. We are a nation ripped apart at the seams, and for what reason?"

"Because of those greedy rebels and their slaves!" someone yelled from the back of the crowd.

"Slavery, yes," the man on the stump stated. This guy oozed calm. "But also tariffs. And a different economy. And states' rights. Those Confederate states that seceded? They left our Union because they believe their individual needs are more important than the needs of the whole."

"Selfish morons!" someone else from the crowd yelled, and a bunch of the adults chuckled.

The important man didn't laugh, no, sir. He shot a look of ice in the direction of the comment. "They believe in their cause as much as we believe in ours. Which is why this is going to be a war like none the world has ever seen."

The crowd cheered and waved things in the air at that, but Johnny felt like maybe they hadn't heard him right.

"We know in our hearts that the Union must survive. We are a nation built on differences. But we are only strong *together*."

Another cheer from the crowd, and this time Johnny cheered, too.

"And so I present to you"—the man swept his palm over the troops who had assembled in one corner of the square—"the Third Ohio Volunteer Regiment. I am Captain Leonidas McDougal, and it is my highest honor to lead these men into battle. It is my highest honor to do everything in my God-given power to keep this nation whole! *The Union must be preserved!*"

With that, he leapt off the stump. Bugles blasted through the air like triumphant eagles, brassy and showy, not sneaky like the power of that drum. The crowd cheered, rose petals rained down from above, and people swarmed to press gifts like combs, pocketknives, cigars, and slippers into the hands of the departing soldiers.

The Union must be preserved.

Johnny nodded.

His help was obviously needed.

Johnny stood on tiptoe to spot the important man, Captain McDougal. The captain swung up on a horse several feet away. Johnny pushed back through the maze of belt buckles and ribbons until he stood beside the captain's mount.

"Captain McDougal!" Johnny yelled up to him.

The captain didn't hear him. The officer winked at a nearby girl in a frilly pink dress.

"Captain McDougal!" Johnny yelled louder.

The captain turned in Johnny's direction but looked over his head to the crowd behind him.

"Down here!"

At last, Captain McDougal saw him.

"Captain, sir!" Johnny saluted. "My name is John Joseph Clem, and I volunteer my services to the Third Ohio Regiment, sir!"

As Johnny stood there, chest puffed out and arm stiffened in salute, he felt Captain Leonidas McDougal scan all four feet, forty pounds of him. The captain's mouth ticked up.

And then the captain laughed. Full-on, head-tilted-back, belly-clutching laughed.

"I'm not enlisting infants, son."

The captain dug his heels into the side of his horse and trotted away, stirring up a cloud of dust.

Johnny coughed.

Infant?

Infantry, maybe.

"I'll show him," Johnny muttered.

CHAPTER 2

The big, bold drum overtook the thumping in Johnny's chest again, and all those proud fellas in their crisp blue uniforms filed toward the train station. Ladies wept, men hurrahed, and kids ran alongside the ranks, pumping fists in the air and doling out wisdom like "Hit those rebels right between the eyes!"

Johnny wanted to follow that beating drum more than he'd ever wanted anything.

Instead, he followed Pop down the dusty road home, kicking up a rock here and there and muttering nasty words under his breath.

Pop stopped, waited. "Why the long face, John Joseph? I thought that spectacle would cheer you."

"I volunteered for the regiment, but the captain laughed at me."

Pop's face twisted. "You volunteered? Don't be ridiculous."

Boy, did that ever get Johnny red. "Pop, if you say I can, they'll let me join the army. I'll sign up on one of those thirty-day stints. Surely we'll whup those rebels in a month's time! I just need you to say I can, and the army will let me in."

Pop's face twisted in the opposite direction, from smirk to scowl. "John Joseph, you're a child! That's ridiculous."

That was the second time he called Johnny that, *ridiculous*. Johnny couldn't hold it in. All the anger he'd bottled up over the last couple of months came spewing out.

"You know what's ridiculous, Pop? You. Working on those trains. *Still*. After everything. Don't that kinda make you Mama's killer?"

Johnny had barely finished saying it when Pop's open hand flew out and—*smack!*—landed square on his cheek. It burned hotter than Johnny's anger.

"Don't you *ever* say that to me again, John Joseph,"

Pop hissed. "You go to church right now and ask forgiveness for talking to your father that way."

"But, Pop—"

"Now!" Pop pointed back downtown, in the direction of the church. "On your knees, son!"

Johnny's shoulders fell. He headed toward church.
He wasn't about to argue with his pop on this one.
But he was nowhere near giving up, neither.

Johnny stood across the street from the Catholic church.
A small cross sat atop the building. "I'm sorry for what
I'm about to do," he whispered. "But I don't see any
other way."

Johnny's little brother, Louis, nudged his shoulder.
Johnny hated that Louis was already as big as him.
"Whatcha doing?" Louis said.

Johnny sighed. He wasn't surprised that Louis and
their sister, Lizzie, showed up, but it would've been a
lot easier if they hadn't. "Praying."

Louis laughed. "You need it, from what I hear. Pop
sent me and Lizzie to come to church with you."

Lizzie bounced on her toes behind Louis. "Can I

light one of the candles for Mama today, John Joseph? Louis got to do it last time."

Johnny knelt on the ground beside her and put his hands on her shoulders. "All right. But hey—"

Johnny swallowed. There was no way he could allow himself to cry right now. No turning back.

"I'm going swimming in the canal instead, okay?" And then he added, "Don't tell Pop," because he knew then for sure they'd tell.

"You're going to get in so much trouble," Louis sang.

"Maybe," Johnny muttered, and stood. "Go on in, okay? I'll deal with Pop . . . later."

Lizzie frowned and shook her curls, and it about broke Johnny's heart in half. "You're not telling the truth, John Joseph. I'm gonna light a candle for you, too."

Johnny blinked because he couldn't have tears. "That's a good idea, Lizzie."

The two headed in through the big wooden doors.

Johnny pretended to head to the canal.

———— ✦ ————

On the train platform, those awful wheels stood perfectly still. It was the first time Johnny had ever really *looked* at train wheels. Before the accident, he'd never thought to look. And after, there was no way he'd give them his attention as they whizzed by.

They were *massive*—twice Johnny's height, at least, each of them inches thick. They joined forces using long, strong iron bars and cogs and bolts. Of course they would crush whatever fell in their path. Horrible, awful, nasty things, train wheels.

Johnny shuddered, breaking out in a cold sweat. "You're such a baby, John Joseph," he told himself. "Soldiers ride on trains."

A quick glance around the platform told Johnny no one had noticed him—they were too busy weeping and hugging their loved ones to see him at the edge

A United States military locomotive from 1865. This rail car belonged to President Lincoln. *[LC-DIG-ppmsca-08257]*

of the station, sweating and swearing to himself. He quickly counted to thirteen, his lucky number. Counting to thirteen was like his own private tempo; Johnny liked that it was an odd number that most people shied away from. He realized now, after hearing that drum this morning, that counting sounded like a drumbeat in his head: *onetwothree fourfivesix seveneightnine ten-eleventwelve THIRTEEN.*

With slick palms, Johnny grabbed the bars alongside the train steps and climbed aboard.

He spat down onto the wheel for good measure.

The train car was packed with soldiers shuffling baggage, soldiers clapping one another's backs, soldiers leaning out windows to kiss pretty ladies. But weaving through the crowd was a man wearing a black hat with a shiny brass nameplate and an official-looking bow tie. The train conductor.

Johnny had to hide—and quick! The conductor smiled, thumped a few fellas on their backs, and helped a guy shove his overstuffed knapsack onto the wooden rack overhead. With each movement, he got closer, closer. . . .

Johnny's only chance was to stay low. He dove under a nearby seat and lay flat. A soldier sat down just after, and his feet and the feet of the others on the bench hid Johnny well enough.

The conductor passed into the next car.

"All aboard!" the conductor shouted. The soldiers stamped their boots on the metal floor of the train as the engine chugged to life. From under the seat, the sound was deafening.

The train lurched forward. Every bone in Johnny's body jarred. Where he hid, he was likely right on top

of one of those awful, monstrous wheels. Bile crept up his throat.

"So long, Newark!" one of the soldiers yelled. "We gotta go nab us some rebs!"

The soldiers cheered.

Johnny counted to thirteen.

CHAPTER 3

On a bed of pain and anguish
Lay dear Annie Lisle,
Chang'd were the lovely features
Gone the happy smile.

Johnny's mother used to sing that.

His mother had an awful singing voice but a huge heart, and so she warbled songs in her horrible voice like she was a regular songbird.

When Johnny was little, it used to embarrass him in church, her singing like that.

He'd give anything to hear her awful singing right now.

Instead, he was curled up under a train seat between six sets of smelly feet, rattling toward war, listening to men belt out deep-voiced army tunes, riding on top of the thing that killed her.

Johnny hated train wheels.

He almost wished he would be found so he could think of anything else but those dadgummed wheels and her fragile body.

Johnny's stomach wanted to flop open and spill its contents. He wanted to shout, "Hey! Lookee under here! A stowaway!" For hours, he fought back both vomit and shouting. *Hours.*

Until, finally, those huge, loud wheels screeched to a stop. Johnny thought the squeals might split his eardrums open. Still, he'd never heard anything so sweet.

"Here we are, fellows!" a voice shouted. "Covington, Kentucky. Welcome to your new home!"

A new home sounded mighty nice to Johnny.

———✦———

Johnny stayed curled up under that seat until the boots had all stamped off the train car and a man had pushed a wide broom up the aisle between seats. Luckily, the man didn't do a very good job, so he swept right on by

Johnny. Johnny sneezed and crawled out, stiff but thankful to finally get off that godforsaken train.

Johnny peeked around the corner of the train door. If he thought the thousand blue uniforms of the Third Ohio had been impressive back in Newark, he wasn't prepared for the many, many thousands of soldiers waiting for orders at this station. Below was a sea of blue wool and brass buttons. Johnny's heart leapt with pride. He'd made the right choice.

Disappearing into the crowd wouldn't be easy, though. Johnny's tan shirt and breeches couldn't have stood out more if he was wearing a Shawnee head-dress. He hopped off the train and snuck through the crowd toward the station. Most times, he could slide through a group of adults like melted butter. But today, a hand grabbed the back of his shirt.

"Boy, you shouldn't be in the middle of this. Go over there to watch." The soldier nudged Johnny in the direction of a group of civilians who'd gathered at the station, toting gifts and flags.

Johnny nodded. That was safest, for now. The little girl next to him bounced on her toes and reminded Johnny so much of Lizzie that he got a lump in his throat. Maybe he didn't make the right choice.

A whistle cut through the noise of shuffling and moving bags. "Sixth New York!" Those fellas who were with the Sixth slung their bags over their shoulders, grabbed the jackets they'd removed in the heat, and pushed toward the edge of the station.

"'Scuse!"

"Pardon me!"

"Move it!"

"Wait, did they say Sixth or Sixtieth?"

"Did my regiment already leave? My regiment didn't leave, did they?"

"That's us, Buck!"

It was chaos.

Johnny watched five or six regiments assemble and leave this way, then a whistle blew and familiar words followed: "Third Ohio!"

It was hot, and with this many fellas packed together, a lot of them had taken off their thick blue wool jackets. This was his shot.

"Sorry, sir," Johnny whispered so quietly, no one could hear him. He lifted a jacket gently off a knapsack and wrapped it around his shoulders. Way he figured, the soldier would be issued another one in no time.

But Johnny, he needed this jacket if he was to serve his country.

Johnny lifted his shoulders to his ears, pushed up the sleeves of this itchy wool coat, and fell into step behind the Third Ohio.

Somewhere up ahead, a drummer pounded a beat that made Johnny's feet step in time: *rrrrrraTAtat, rrrrraTAtat, rrrrratatatatatataTAtatat.*

One thousand and *one* men, marching.

Johnny's regiment.

Yep. He made the right choice.

Three unidentified Union soldiers.
[LC-DIG-ppmsca-37126]

The soldiers hadn't taken more than twenty steps down Main Street when one of the older fellas, maybe twenty years old, looked over his shoulder at Johnny. He was hairier than any guy Johnny had ever seen—hair peeked up from the fella's shirt, out his ears, down from his nostrils. He fell into step with Johnny.

"Hey, Peewee," he said with a smile. "What're you doing here?"

Three of Hairy's buddies fell into step next to Johnny, too.

Johnny didn't stop marching because they didn't stop, and he thought this might be a test. "I'm here to serve my country, sir!"

Those guys didn't laugh, but they shared winks and elbow jabs. "What's your name, then, soldier?" Hairy asked.

"John Jo—" Johnny stopped, cleared his throat. "John Lincoln Clem, sir!"

Hairy's face split into a grin. "Lincoln, huh? Lucky coincidence on your mama's part to name you that."

"No, sir!" Johnny shouted. Boy, this marching and shouting together could wear a set of lungs plum out. Plus, he had trouble not tripping over this too-long jacket. "Nope. I figure if I'm going to fight for the man, I better honor him right. So I changed it. Just now."

Hairy and his buddies laughed long and hard at that and took turns smacking Johnny on the back. It hurt a little, but he didn't let on.

"Lincoln!" one of them said, and laughed.

"If that doesn't beat all!" another shouted.

Hairy leveled his thick eyebrows at Johnny. "And darned if you don't look just like him."

They all had another long laugh at that. It wasn't true; the photographs Johnny had seen of President Lincoln in the newspapers showed him to be tall, gaunt, and dark. Johnny was blond and round. And not at all tall.

Just then, a man on a horse swung back toward the group's laughter.

Captain McDougal.

Drat.

But Hairy and his buddies quickstepped Johnny right into the middle of the pack.

"Howdy, sir!" Hairy shouted up to the captain.

Marching in between the belts of Hairy and his buddies, Johnny couldn't see the captain's face. Plus, the sun was behind him, so the captain was just this bulky, shadowy figure on a horse.

Captain McDougal grunted. "Marching too tight, men. Standard is twenty-eight inches."

"Yes, sir!" Hairy and his buddies barked.

The shadowy captain led his horse away, muttering, "Stupid volunteers don't know a lick about soldiering. . . ."

Johnny's new friends loosened their march around him. Hairy clapped Johnny on the back.

"I like you, Peewee. Name's Harry."

Johnny couldn't help it; he busted out with a laugh. "I coulda guessed."

Harry's buddies laughed, and thank goodness, Harry did, too.

"Stick with us, kid. We'll make sure you get your shot at those rebs."

Johnny grinned ear to ear and kept marching to the beat of the drum: *rrrrrraTAtat, rrrrraTAtat, rrrrratatatatatataTAtatat.* He had a uniform (well, a jacket at least) and some soldier buddies. He was marching to the beat of their same drum. He was part of the army!

Johnny marched for another mile or so with his

new pals, right up to camp alongside the wide, shining Ohio River. The drum stopped playing a marching beat and played a different rhythm: *taptaptap, taptaptap, taptaptap, TAP TAP.*

Johnny knew, somehow, that it meant *stop here.* Somehow, that drum spoke to him and he understood.

The fellas all set down their knapsacks, opened them, and pulled out tents.

It hit Johnny: he didn't have a tent.

He had nothing besides a too-big jacket. No money, no food, no nothing.

He stood there feeling sorry for himself because he didn't have a place to bunk for the night, when the drummer himself came up. The drummer was tall and lean, maybe sixteen years old or so, and he cradled that drum like a baby. Johnny smiled, because boy, did that guy and his drum make him feel like he belonged. Those drumbeats were why Johnny was here.

The drummer narrowed his eyes on Johnny. "What're you doing here?" he growled. "Go home. This isn't child's play."

CHAPTER 4

Johnny blinked at the drummer. "I'm here to serve my country, of course. Just like you."

The drummer leaned in close to Johnny. "I'm here to earn a paycheck, kid. You better start thinking that way, too. This here's a *job*. The army isn't your nanny." He stormed off.

Johnny supposed Harry must've seen the *holy cow* look on his face because Harry thumped him on the back. Johnny coughed but managed to make it sound like a laugh.

"Tell you what, Peewee," Harry said, arm slung over Johnny's shoulder. Johnny was one of the guys with Harry. "I'll let you bunk with me tonight if you

put up this here tent for me." He toed a musty gray pile of canvas.

"Right away, sir!"

Harry smiled. He sat in the shade of a nearby tree and guzzled the contents of his canteen. It didn't smell like water in there, neither.

"Let me tell you about the girl I left behind, Peewee. . . ." Harry went into this big story of a girl named Amalie who was prettier than "a fresh-dug outhouse with the softest-ever newsprint." Johnny didn't see how that was pretty at all, but Harry had himself a good laugh.

Pretty soon, the camp doctor came around. "Gentlemen," he said. Harry scrambled to his feet and stood next to Johnny in front of the pile of canvas.

"Yes, sir!"

Doc looked over his spectacles at the duo. He might've glanced an extra second at Johnny, but it was hard to tell, he was so old and squinty-eyed.

"You boys in good health?"

"Yes, sir!"

"You telling the truth?"

"Yes, sir!"

"Step forward."

Johnny and Harry did.

That doc may have been old, but he pulled his fingers tight into a fist and—*pap! pap!*—punched Johnny and Harry both square in the chest. Johnny sucked in a breath. Even Harry panted a bit.

"Pass. Both of you. Carry on."

"I passed the army medical exam?" Johnny asked Harry.

Harry shrugged.

"I passed the army medical exam!"

Harry waved his hand over the crumpled tent. "Carry on," he said, and continued comparing his girlfriend to toilets and laughing at himself.

Johnny watched the others putting up their tents and figured out that the middle pole had to go up first. Pretty soon, he had staked that tent down perfectly, the fabric so tight you could bounce a button off it.

"Not bad, Peewee," Harry said, and lifted his canteen at Johnny. "Not bad. Tell you what. You can bunk with me if—"

"Wow! Thanks, sir!"

"I'm not finished. If you carry *your* fair share of *my* chores." He stuck out his hand for a handshake.

Johnny knew a good pact when he saw one. "Deal," he said, and they shook hands.

It hurt a little, but not as much as the medical exam, so Johnny didn't show it.

So that's how it went for the next couple of weeks. Johnny fetched firewood and heavy pails of water. He cleaned garbage out of tents and shoveled horse manure. Meanwhile, Harry and the boys of the Third Ohio would drill, looking (Johnny thought) like clowns in a traveling show, the way they kept getting their orders mixed up and turning about-face when they should've turned right wheel. They'd laugh and complain about the heat and take too-long breaks, while Captain McDougal snarled, "You boys aren't used to denying yourselves much, are you?"

And for that, they earned thirteen dollars a month. Thirteen whole dollars! Some of them, like that nasty drummer boy—his name was William—wanted that handsome salary more than a restored Union. Johnny didn't much care for those fellas. And since he wasn't enlisted, he didn't get paid.

Camp was nice. The fellas gave Johnny his own knife and fork, tin plate, tin cup, and tin spoon. He had a canteen and a sleeping pallet on the dirt. He had adventure and glory and pride.

Pride most of all.

Sometime into the third week at camp, Harry came across a pair of scissors. (Johnny didn't ask how.) He hung a placard, HAIRCUTS, TEN CENTS, and boy, did those soldiers line up. Harry handed the scissors to Johnny and told him he'd give him a penny a cut.

Johnny hacked away at hair for hours, and he got pretty dadgummed good at it.

Until William sat in the chair.

"Just a little off the back, Runt."

Johnny cut so close to his scalp, William looked darned near bald. Harry and his buddies roared with laughter.

Johnny didn't get paid for that one.

He thought it was his best cut of the day.

But Johnny still loved that drum William played. When he played, Johnny closed his eyes and let the drumbeats rumble through his chest. He couldn't hear a drum and *not* stand a little taller, lift his chin a little higher.

Harry knew that to Johnny, the army was more than a job. He must've. Because late one day, after he'd been drilling for hours in the hot June sun, Harry approached Johnny, wearing a smile wider than the Ohio River. Tufts of hair stuck out from all over his face when he smiled like that.

"I've got a surprise for you, Peewee."

He swung one arm around from behind his back.

A uniform! A blue Union uniform!

"For . . . me?" Johnny whispered. He could hardly keep the tears back, but he had to or else he'd never hear the end of it from the fellas.

"Yep. Try it on."

He did. It was a little rumpled and too big, but it was *his uniform*.

"We had it cut down by the regiment's tailor."

"We?"

"Yeah. Me and the guys."

Johnny swallowed a smile. The fellas made him a uniform.

"Hey! Check the pockets, too, Peewee."

He did. Inside was some paper.

No, not paper.

Money!

"Thirteen dollars, just like the rest of us," Harry said. "We took a collection, see. It's your salary."

"My salary? You guys don't need to pay me for helping out. You already feed me."

"Nah, Peewee," Harry said. "You don't understand."

And that's when Harry swung his *other* arm from behind his back.

"A drum?"

Harry's grin just about split his face in two. "The

regiment needs another drummer boy. The guys and I think it should be you."

He handed over the drum.

"Me?"

Johnny swallowed, turning the drum in his hands.

Boy, what a dandy! A double-headed tubular snare drum, bright red. A fierce eagle clutching an American shield surrounded by stars was painted on its side. The skins stretched across it were cool and tight, and the shoulder strap sat snug on Johnny's collarbone when he wriggled into it.

He tapped it lightly with a dirty fingernail.

Prrrrm.

Like a pulse.

"My drum!"

A Union drum displayed at the Soldiers and Sailors National Military Museum and Memorial in Pittsburgh, Pennsylvania. *[Wikimedia Commons, author Daderot]*

CHAPTER 5

The drum didn't seem heavy when Johnny first hefted it, but after three or four hours of lugging it around, its eight pounds felt more like a boulder. And because it was worn slung to the left hip and bounced when marching, he got a big, shiny purple bruise on his left thigh. The cotton sling rubbed the back of his neck darn near bloody raw. And he learned quick not to tap the animal hide by flexing his wrists, because, *ouch*, those rosewood drumsticks were heavy.

"Drum from your shoulders, you idiot," William would yell, and then he'd whup Johnny upside the head. "And don't stoop—you'll wear your back out before you turn double digits." (Johnny didn't know how William found out he was nine. He hadn't told a soul.)

For the Third Ohio, it was just Johnny and William as drummers. They trained with all the other drummers camped out in Covington, Kentucky, but the other fellas lumped the two of them together, WilliamandJohnny, like they were brothers or something. It made Johnny miss his real brother, Louis, something fierce, because when Louis whupped him, Johnny whupped him back.

A Union drum corps from 1863.
[LC-DIG-cwpb-04019]

But still, Johnny loved it. That drum had *power*.

The Union soldiers stomped the lush green grass into brown dust on the patch of ground beside the Ohio River. The drummers trained there, along with the infantry and cavalry and artillery from all the regiments. The troops hadn't seen any rebels yet, though, and the boys were restless to fight.

"When're we gonna get to fire these things, Captain?" Harry would shake his musket and yell at Captain McDougal when the captain made inspections. The captain would glare at him and say, "I hope you never do."

Once, Johnny asked Harry what he thought the captain meant by that, and Harry just waved him off. "That guy? He's just trying to make sure we're really serious about this soldiering stuff, that's all. He doesn't care for those of us who volunteered to fight, see. We haven't had the right training, he says. Which is nonsense, if you ask me. Anyone can point a gun and shoot. Nah, captain likes them army born-and-bred, like you, Peewee." The two shared a good laugh.

Maybe a week or so after Johnny got his drum, the musicians heard some rustling nearby while they were practicing. "Shhh!" William said, and hushed the drum group by slashing his drumstick toward a nearby scrub bush. "Over there!"

The bushes moved!

"A rebel," he whispered. Johnny felt his eyes widen. William quietly stepped out of his drum sling. "Keep drumming," he ordered the others, "and I'll go nab him!" Johnny nodded and *taptaptapp*ed away with the others.

William tiptoed into the bushes. "Aha!" he shouted, and dove in.

Johnny swallowed. *Our first prisoner!* he thought.

The bushes rustled like mad, then William stumbled out of them, dusting his breeches and spewing curse words.

"You okay, William?" Johnny asked.

"Where is he? Where's that reb?" another fella asked.

"You didn't let him get away, did you?"

The bushes rustled again, and a rib-thin dog trotted out, tail wagging. The brown-and-white mutt loped over to William and sat at his feet. His big brown eyes stared up at William's red face, and his tongue lolled out to the side.

"Go on, now," William yelled down at the dog. "Git!" He stomped his foot.

The dog wagged his tail so hard, his whole body twisted.

The boys all hooted and howled with laughter.

"There's your prisoner, Will!"

"What a catch!"

"We should call him Reb!"

By the time Johnny and the others gave Reb a scratch behind his ears and a pat on his rump, he wasn't leaving for nothing. But he was all eyes for William.

That evening, when the musicians headed back for supper, Reb followed on William's heels. Every five or ten steps, William would turn to glare at him. Reb panted and wagged his tail.

Reb sat next to William at supper, and even though the rest of the fellas snuck him scraps, he wouldn't leave William's side. Johnny thought that dog sure had poor taste.

Harry clapped William on the back. "Captain

McDougal sees you with that dog, and you'll be wearing the barrel shirt for sure. You can't keep that mutt."

"I don't want to keep him," William said between gritted teeth.

But Johnny knew it was all for show, all just because William was embarrassed he hadn't captured a rebel. Johnny knew because he caught William behind a tent, scratching Reb's belly. "You can't stay here, got it, fella? This isn't a good place for a dog."

But William didn't stop scratching, and the dog didn't leave.

That night, with Reb curled up at William's feet by the blazing campfire, the other musicians and Johnny played a nighttime ditty, like they did every night. They'd just wrapped up a loud round of "Brave Boys Are They!" when they heard an extra drumbeat:

TiptipTAPTAP.

"Shhh!" William called, holding up a drumstick.

"You hear another rebel in the bushes there, Will?" Harry joked. The fellas all laughed.

TiptipTAPTAP.

"That wasn't ours," Johnny muttered, and he played it back into the starry night: *tiptipTAPTAP.*

TippetytippetytappetyTAP was the next beat.

TippetytippetytappetyTAP Johnny played in response.

TAPTAPTAP. TAPTAPTAP. TAPTAPTAP. BOOM!

Johnny played it, too: *TAPTAPTAP. TAPTAPTAP. TAPTAPTAP. BOOM!*

Harry's eyes narrowed. "Hear that, boys?" He cracked his hairy knuckles. "Those rebels are close by!"

———◦◦◦◦◦———

Johnny hardly slept that night, partly because he was nervous about those rebels camped so close by but more because they'd finally get to see some *action*! For weeks, they'd done nothing but train and march, march and train. Johnny was so impatient to get this war under way, it felt like ten thousand pins were pricking him.

But he must've somehow drifted off to sleep, because he woke up to a noise so thunderous, so booming, it sounded like the earth was cracking in two.

Confederate fire!

Johnny about jumped out of his skin.

"Grab your drum, Peewee!" Harry yelled, bounding into his uniform. "We're gonna need your drum calls!"

Johnny had just enough time to slide on his

uniform jacket over his long johns and slip into his drum sling before Captain McDougal's voice rang through camp:

"Move it, boys! Grab your weapons! Get me a drummer boy!"

Shells and cannon fire lit the camp briefly, like flashes of lightning. The booms and blasts that followed rattled Johnny's teeth. Through the scattered blazes of light and the clods of dirt raining down on him, Johnny scrambled to find Captain McDougal. He saluted the captain. The captain scowled down at him.

"Those Confederates aren't fighting like gentlemen, attacking us here," he said. "You ready?"

"Yes, sir!"

A bomb exploded nearby, shaking Johnny from the heels up.

Johnny's heart raced as shells blasted around him. Chunks of earth and rock flew all around, stinging his skin as the debris pelted him. The smell of gunpowder hung in the air. The Union boys ducked between tents and scuttled about, trying to figure out where to gather.

"Call the Assembly, boy. *Now.*"

Johnny's hands shook.

Taptaptap, taptaptap, taptaptap, TAP TAP.

He played it over and over again. His small but powerful drum could be heard above the explosions: *taptaptap, taptaptap, taptaptap, TAP TAP.*

The boys followed the beats and assembled in long lines, ready to fight.

A flash of fire was followed by a boom so loud, Johnny could feel it in the hollow of his bones.

Men fell.

"Good, son," Captain McDougal said. He still *said,* rather than *shouted.* "Call the Double Quickstep Advance."

"The Advance, the Advance . . ." Johnny muttered to himself. Shells exploded all around. Smoke drifted into his eyes, stinging them and burning his nose and throat. His ears rang from the nearby explosions, making him dizzy. He tried counting to his lucky number thirteen to calm himself down. But counting to thirteen and drumming regular beats didn't mix—he couldn't think of the Advance.

"The Advance!" Captain McDougal hissed.

More fire and smoke and gunpowder and rumble.

Men moaned.

Johnny's hands were so sweaty, he was afraid he might drop his drumsticks.

Prrrrt-trp-trp-tippy-tippy-trp-trp, prrrrt-trp-trp-tippy-tippy-trp-trp came the Long Roll from behind him.

William stood, chin lifted, and drummed the Long Roll, the Advance.

The Union men charged, whooping and hollering.

The blue uniforms ran into the explosions. Some dropped to their knees. Some wore horrible, twisted faces. Some had wide, terrified eyes.

"Left Wheel," the captain ordered.

William played the call.

The smoke grew thicker, choking Johnny. He heard one Union boy yell, "The rebs ain't in regular uniforms, boys! Shoot at anyone not wearing blue!"

Flashing lights blinded him. Exploding cannon fire rattled his brain around inside his skull.

Men littered the ground.

The smoke grew thicker still. So thick Johnny's stomach churned with the stuff. So thick he barely saw William, still standing behind him.

But he heard that drum.

Everyone heard that drum.

William beat out every call flawlessly.

And then, as quickly as it started, it stopped. A few more pops and cracks, but the firing ceased.

"Call the Retreat," Captain McDougal ordered.

Tappitytappitytappity.

The Union men returned.

Most of them did, anyway.

Their faces were all sweat and grime, their eyes red from dust and smoke. They coughed and gagged and cried. They bled. Johnny couldn't tell if the tears were from smoke or something else.

Johnny's tears were from something else.

There were men—*Union men*—dead.

And he'd put his regiment in danger. He'd hesitated because he was scared.

He'd failed his troops.

CHAPTER 6

Weeks passed, and the weather got cold. It matched Johnny's mood; he hadn't forgiven himself for letting down the troops. Harry told him that he hadn't let anyone down, that most of the boys who'd been shot in the skirmish hadn't died.

But two of them had.

An icy November snap blew in off the Ohio River. The soldiers shivered next to the dwindling campfire.

"Johnny," Captain McDougal said, blowing into his cupped hands. "Sound the Wood Call."

Johnny wanted to roll his eyes, but no way would he do that in front of the captain. It wasn't that the troops didn't need wood—they did. They needed lots of wood.

They'd built small shacks for winter quarters, and they'd used logs to make walkways across ice and mud. But wood was still needed for cooking and heat, and the surrounding area was darn near cleaned out. So anytime Johnny sounded the Wood Call on his drum, the others would gripe and moan because it meant miles of walking to find dry, thick logs. The fellas *hated* that call.

But instead of letting the captain down again, Johnny shimmied into his drum sling and sounded the Wood Call. Sure enough, the fellas groaned out of their shacks, some of them chucking clods of mud at him.

Those were the kinds of calls the captain asked him to drum after the skirmish.

Johnny gathered wood, too. There wasn't a thing the fellas did that he didn't do. He wouldn't let down his regiment again. He found mostly sticks.

Harry went around and gathered his required amount of wood by convincing some of the other fellas to remove the signs they'd hung above the doorways of their shacks. It was a good idea, and soon the fellas were tossing those signs onto the fire: BUZZARD'S ROOST and SWINE HOTEL and HOLE IN THE WALL.

That afternoon, with the fire roaring again and the boys drinking out of a jug given to them from a nearby farmer, the mood got warm again. William even showed off the latest trick he'd taught Reb: He'd shoot at Reb with his finger and yell, "Bang! Bang! Shot you, Reb!" The dog would drop to his side, tongue lolling. The fellas howled. They loved that dog. But they *didn't* love that the dog shared the food supply.

"Johnny!" Harry yelled through the campfire smoke. His voice was thick, and he tossed his musket at Johnny.

Johnny caught it, but BOY, was it heavy!

"Go nab us a rabbit, Johnny!" Harry shouted. At the mention of meat, Johnny's stomach growled. The troops hadn't had real meat in weeks—only that awful salt horse, which tasted as good as its name.

Johnny smiled to beat all. "Really, Harry? You'll let me fire it?" he said, swinging the barrel of the musket Harry's way.

Harry ducked. "Easy, there, trigger! Fire at rabbits only."

The musket was an 1853 Enfield, sleek and solid and longer than Johnny was tall. He practically

An 1853 Enfield Rifle-Musket—the second most widely used firearm of the Civil War.

skipped out of camp, or would've, if he could've while hauling that heavy gun. As he left, Johnny heard Harry guffaw, "How much we betting he comes back with a handful of walnuts?"

Johnny shook his head. That guy. "Don't take that bet," Johnny yelled back over his shoulder. The fellas laughed again.

Johnny was only about three-quarters of a mile away from camp when he heard it: a rustling in the bushes. His mind jumped to Reb, William's dog. But no, he didn't leave camp without William. He wouldn't be out there.

Then he thought: *It's an* actual *rebel!* His heart raced. The bushes rustled again.

Calm down, you sissy, Johnny told himself. *It's a rabbit. Rebels wouldn't be back up here again, not after they saw how many of us are camped here.*

He hefted the wooden butt of the musket against his shoulder. His arms burned with the strain, the gun was so solid. He poked aside some leafless branches with the barrel of the gun, hoping to get a clean shot, so the fellas wouldn't be eating rabbit with a bunch of minié balls buried in the meat.

A young slave boy, photographed in 1862.

[Yale Collection of American Literature, Beinecke Rare Book and Manuscript Library]

"Don't shoot!"

Johnny leapt backward and dropped the musket. By the time he swept it back up out of the mud, a boy had come out of the bushes.

A Negro boy.

His clothes were rags, and Johnny shivered just looking at how thin they were. The boy was tall and skinny—very skinny. He had thick hair matted with mud, and his large brown eyes looked like they could see things Johnny's couldn't.

The boy took a step forward. Johnny raised the barrel of the musket at him.

"Don't shoot," the boy said again calmly. "I'm not a rebel."

"That's plain to see."

The fella didn't raise his hands or run. He just stood there, looking tired and cold and muddy.

That's when Johnny saw his neck.

An iron collar gripped it tight. Long metal arms arched off the collar, and bells dangled off the end of each arm. The bells were coated with mud, though, so their tinkling was muffled.

Johnny waved the musket tip at it. "What's that around your neck?"

The fella didn't pause. "A slave collar."

Johnny swallowed. "You an escaped slave?"

"Yes."

Johnny lowered the gun.

The boy took another step forward.

Johnny snapped the gun up again.

And again, the fella didn't flinch.

How do you not flinch when someone levels a musket at you?

"You used to looking down the barrel of a gun or something?" Johnny asked.

The guy lifted one shoulder, then let it drop.

Johnny lowered the barrel. He couldn't tell how old the fella was. He had the build of somebody fifteen, but the eyes of somebody fifty-five.

"You hungry?" Johnny asked.

The fella nodded.

Johnny jerked his head back toward camp. "Follow me."

———◦◦◦◦———

"Well, well," said Harry, circling Johnny and the escaped slave, back at camp. "You didn't nab a rabbit, Peewee."

Harry smiled, dug in his pocket, came up with some hardtack. He offered his cracker to the fella. "What's your name?"

"Jackson, sir." He took the cracker and nibbled it. He was so skinny, Johnny couldn't understand how he wasn't wolfing it down.

Harry waggled his pinky finger around inside his hairy ear. "So what are we going to do with you . . . ?"

William strode over with Reb at his heels. "No. No way. We aren't going to just *keep* an escaped slave, Harry. He belongs somewhere."

Johnny narrowed his eyes at William. "You treat that dog of yours better than you treat most folks, you know that?"

William crossed his arms over his chest. "It's the law. I'm not going to break the law."

"Break what law?" Captain McDougal asked as he came around the main cabin toward the gathering.

The fellas fell silent. Captain McDougal's gaze fell on Jackson.

Jackson straightened, his wrists and knees and elbows jutting out everywhere. He still wore that hideous iron collar, but he looked Captain McDougal level in the eye. "I'd like to serve the Union army, sir."

William shifted. "But it's against the law, sir. Escaped slaves should be returned. . . ."

Captain McDougal held up his hand, quieting William. Johnny held in a grin.

"That was a law enforced by states that no longer want to be a part of this Union," the captain said to William. "Those laws no longer apply to us. As far as I'm concerned, the Confederates make a law, and I'm going to do the exact opposite."

Johnny couldn't hold back his grin any longer. Harry's eyes lit up and he nodded at the captain.

"Welcome to the regiment, Jackson," Captain McDougal said. He extended his hand. Jackson shook it.

"You over eighteen, son?" the captain asked him.

"Yes, sir," Jackson said. It was the first time since Johnny met him that he looked sheepish.

Captain McDougal scanned the crowd, and his eyes lighted on William. "You'll be a drummer. We can't ever have too many drummers."

"But, sir—" William started.

Captain clapped William on the shoulder. "Make sure he gets a drum and some sticks." He wheeled about and headed to his cabin.

William glared at Jackson. "I have an extra drum that needs repair and no sticks. And I'm *not* training you. It's bad enough I have *him*," he spat at Johnny. William whipped around and stomped away, Reb bounding after him.

A young drummer boy believed to be a freed or escaped slave.
[National Archives]

"I don't know what that dog sees in him," Johnny muttered.

Johnny grabbed his drumsticks out of his back

pocket, where he always kept them. "Here," he said, giving them to Jackson.

Jackson shook his head. "I can't pay you for them."

Johnny shrugged. "Nah, it's a loan. I've got money. I'll buy more when the supply wagon rolls around."

Jackson rolled the drumsticks between his fingers. The corners of his mouth turned up. "A drummer," he whispered. "For the Union."

Yep, Johnny thought. *This guy and I will get along just fine.*

CHAPTER 7

Getting up early stank. Johnny woke about five thirty every morning to the Drummer's Call, sounded by whoever was orderly drummer that week: *ttttTAPTAP-TAP ttttTAPTAPTAP ttttTAPTAPTAP*. The weeks Johnny was the orderly drummer, he got up even earlier.

He shrugged into his uniform, grabbed his drum and new sticks, and met the other musicians at the edge of camp. They'd play Reveille to wake the others at six a.m., drumming and marching throughout camp. Reveille was made up of stroke rolls: *tickatickaticka-TICK tickaTICK tickaTICK, tickatickatickaTICK ticka-TICK tickaTICK*. A loud, get-stirring kind of beat.

The fellas hated the drummers for waking them,

especially the fellas who'd stayed up late singing songs by the campfire the night before. They'd moan and halfheartedly throw things at the musicians. "I was dreaming of my girl back home, you scoundrel!"

Johnny would dash to breakfast then, which was never a meal like fresh eggs with coffee, the kind he'd have at home. No, this was usually a big pot of mush, and if they were lucky, they'd get a dollop of honey on top to cut the bland taste. But it was warm and belly-filling, and because Johnny was there first, they never ran out before they got to him. Because most days they did run out.

About seven a.m., the musicians would march around camp again, playing the Breakfast Call, "Peas Upon a Trencher." The other fellas would come eat, and the musicians—several drummers, two buglers, and a fife player—would prepare for the day. One of the musicians would post the practice schedule near the main cabin so the infantry fellas wouldn't get confused when they heard a call like Assemble or the Alarm roll through camp. Otherwise, they might take up arms and start shooting. Nobody wanted that kind of mistake.

And then the musicians would practice. They'd muffle the sound of the drums by cramming thin strips of leather in the web of snares on the drum.

"Tighten your drum, Johnny!" William barked. "It sounds like you're pounding a dead fish!"

So Johnny would pull down the ears, the leather pieces hanging over the side of the drum, and tighten the knots. It sounded better.

William wouldn't be so irritating if he wasn't right so much.

"Proper posture!" he'd yell, whacking Johnny's back

A Union drum corps from 1863 in the midst of practice.
[LC-DIG-cwpb-04015]

with his drumstick. "Elbows at your side! You must keep a twenty-eight-inch pace! Twenty-eight!"

It was awful hard for a guy Johnny's size to keep regulation pace, but he sure hustled to try.

And if William was mean to Johnny, he was downright nasty to Jackson. He'd point to the place where the slave collar had rubbed Jackson raw before the fellas had removed it with huge tools. "Can't you cover up that scar? No soldier should have to look at that. Disgusting."

Johnny thought Jackson's scar was disgusting, too, but for a different reason than William did. Funny how you can agree with a fella and still disagree with him.

The drummers learned stroke rolls and double stroke rolls, flams, paradiddles, flamadiddles, ruffs, and single and double drags. They learned how to march and play at the same time, which was harder than it looked. They built up strong muscles in their shoulders and back and hands.

Jackson didn't know the technical stuff of drums—things like 6/8 time and beats per minute. But he could play every single roll after watching the others play it two or three times. He was tall, and he could march as straight as a board. And he never forgot a call. Never.

Johnny hoped that some of Jackson's never-forgetting talent might rub off on him.

———————

When the musicians weren't practicing, they were mostly trying to find food and water. The troops were under strict orders not to pillage the nearby Kentucky towns for food or supplies, even the homes that flew Confederate flags.

"Soon these towns will be a part of our glorious Union again," Captain McDougal reminded the fellas. "Do you think they'd be pleased to rejoin us if we steal from them?"

It made sense.

Except that one day.

It was cold—so cold Johnny hadn't taken off his coat in a week, and boy, did it smell like it. He was looking for water, which was a hard enough task on its own, but add in the fact that most of the water was frozen solid and had to be chipped apart before he could get to the liquid stuff? Well, the chore was a knuckle bleeder, that's for sure.

Johnny was hauling a heavy wooden bucket down the

path back to camp when he saw it: the most beautiful, fat pink pig he'd ever laid eyes on.

His stomach growled just looking at those flabby, fleshy hindquarters. The troops hadn't had real, true meat in weeks. Johnny thought he'd gotten used to being hungry. His stomach argued with him, looking at that pig.

It wasn't a wild pig—no fangs, and it was way too fat for that.

"Got out of your pen, did ya?" Johnny whispered. The pig rooted around, found a patch of wild onions, and snarfed them up.

Johnny made a decision right then to have that pig for supper.

But he didn't have a gun.

Lucky for him, Johnny knew Harry was out of the cabin, looking for water, too. Johnny ditched the bucket of water, snuck past the pig, and ran to his quarters. Harry's gun was where he always left it: hanging on a nail above his bunk. Loaded with a single shot.

The pig was even closer to camp than when Johnny had left it. It was like the critter was begging to be supper. So Johnny leveled that gun and whispered, "Sorry I'm breaking the rules." And then he fired.

Flesh and pig blood splattered. Johnny's empty stomach lurched.

But the pig didn't drop, no, sir. No, it turned to Johnny with fury in its eyes. The pig's nostrils flared, it lowered its huge skull, and it charged!

Johnny jumped aside. The pig crashed into a small tree. Johnny didn't have another round for the musket, or else he'd shoot the devil again. The pig was *fast*, too. Back home, Johnny had heard horror stories of people getting stampeded by pigs in a pen, with nothing but their bones left behind once the frenzy stopped. He wasn't sure if this was the same sort of thing, but he wasn't willing to find out. He hauled his butt up a tree and sat.

That pig was ready to cause Johnny the same kind of pain Johnny had caused it. The pig ramrodded the tree over and over again with its thick head, snorting and snuffling hot pig breath up at Johnny. Each time the pig rammed the tree, Johnny gripped the trunk and pictured the tree falling over, pictured *him* becoming the *pig's* supper.

But at last, the wound and the skull pounding caught up with the huge beast. The pig swayed and flopped on its side. It let out one last grunt, and then the light in its eyes dulled.

Johnny hopped out of the tree. Now: How to get this thing back to camp, along with the musket and the bucket of water?

Harry.

When Johnny led Harry back to the pig, Harry licked his lips and clapped him on the back. "Peewee, you are going to be in *so much trouble*. But I sure am glad about it."

Johnny smiled. "Help me get it back to camp."

Harry shook his head. "No way. Captain's already got his eye on me. I'll carry the water and the gun. *Which*, don't ever take again, you little thief."

"But—"

"Take off your coat," Harry said. Johnny did, and shivered. "I'll help you roll the pig onto it. You can drag it in from here."

The two pushed and shoved Johnny's coat under that big, fat pig. For the next hour, Johnny tugged and pulled with all his might until he finally got the pig to the edge of camp.

When the fellas saw Johnny, they dropped their pickup game of one cat and two cats, and boy, did they cheer! But they quickly realized how much trouble he'd be in if he got caught. They decided to build a spit and cook this pig right there, on the outskirts of camp, to avoid getting caught with what was obviously a neighbor's pig.

Ahhhhh, the smell of roasting pig! Sweet and smoky, it wafted all through camp and filled the nostrils of every man out there. They soon had a crowd. They hoped Captain McDougal wasn't in it.

Hours later, the pig was almost cooked, and Captain McDougal still hadn't shown up. Johnny couldn't believe his good luck! One of the fellas was slicing apart the pork with his bowie knife when silence fell over the chatty crowd.

The sea of soldiers parted. Johnny swallowed and prepared to face the wrath of Captain McDougal. But.

Oh no.

It wasn't Captain McDougal.

"General Doolittle," Harry said. He snapped to attention and saluted the old guy, so Johnny did the same.

The general!

Way, way higher rank than captain.

Johnny felt sick.

The general looked from the pig to the crowd of hungry soldiers. His nostrils twitched.

"This isn't a wild pig," he said.

Johnny shook his head.

"No, sir," Harry said.

The general turned to Harry. "You kill this pig, soldier?"

Harry's eyes shot to Johnny. "I did."

No. Johnny wouldn't let Harry take the fall on this one. He felt like he might lose the contents of his stomach (which contained nothing, not even pig yet). But he stepped forward.

"Sir," Johnny said. "He didn't kill that pig. I did."

The general's blue eyes narrowed under his bushy gray eyebrows in a way that made Johnny shiver. "You took a civilian's property."

Johnny's brain whirred. That pig almost killed him, and here he wouldn't even get a taste of it! "But, General," he said. "You wouldn't let a rebel pig bite *you*, would you?"

The general's thick mustache twitched. He inhaled deeply, which might have been a sigh, but appeared to be more like a pretaste of barbeque.

"I get some ribs," he said.

Wow! The hurrah that went up from the boys after that!

They feasted that night on greasy, fatty pig. Johnny sucked the bones, sucked his fingers. Everyone else did, too.

"Thank you, General," the boys said, lifting their tin cups to him.

"That was delicious."

"Best pig I ever ate."

Johnny beamed. "Yeah, thank you, General!"

The general tossed a bone aside, and William's dog, Reb, jumped on it. "Don't thank me yet, Johnny. You haven't faced your punishment."

———◦◦◦———

The barrel shirt.

It was three holes cut in a barrel: one for a head, two for arms. When most fellas wore the barrel shirt, they had to do their drills in it. They marched around, straining from carrying all that extra weight. But Johnny couldn't even lift the barrel off the ground, so the barrel shirt for him was just sitting in a barrel with his head poking out the top. No movement at all. His neck was rubbed raw on the splintery wood, and his arms were numb from holding them through the side holes. It was awful.

He was pretty far away from the campfire, too, so he was cold, but he was close enough to hear the conversation.

The others around the fire were making bullets. Most of the time, they didn't need to do this; bullets made in factories found their way to the battlefield. But every once in a while, the fellas would gather the stray bullets and make their own lucky stock. They'd melt thin lead bars in pots over the fire. When the lead turned to liquid, they'd pour it into the mold, then dip the whole thing in cold water to harden. Once the bullet cooled, the mold opened like a pair of scissors, and out popped a bullet.

William popped one out of the mold, held it up in the firelight, and kissed it.

"Find your home in a rebel's heart," he said, and laughed. A few others laughed with him. Jackson

A bullet mold.

quietly put his bullet mold aside and walked toward the cabins.

"Hey," Johnny whispered to him through the dark. "Jackson. C'mere."

Jackson looked back at the campfire. The fellas weren't supposed to talk to the guy in the barrel shirt.

"It's okay," Johnny said. "They haven't even looked back here once."

Jackson shrugged and sat on the ground next to the barrel.

"Can you scratch my wrist?" Johnny asked. "The right one, right—*ahhh!* Yes. Thanks, Jackson."

Jackson didn't say anything. But all of a sudden, his face looked angry.

"That William," he said, lifting his chin toward the campfire. "That guy doesn't get it. Some of those Confederates, they're nice folks, you know? They're just trying to do right by their beliefs."

Johnny couldn't believe his ears. "But their beliefs are wrong."

Jackson shrugged. "Well, yeah. Being wrong doesn't mean you deserve a bullet in the heart."

Johnny stretched his neck sidewise. "So . . . why are you here, then? I mean, in the army?"

Jackson's eyes lit up the night. "I got a brother. He's still a slave, see. I don't want to hurt anybody. But I want him to be free. My kid brother. He's only seven. He's got a real shot at being *free.*"

Jackson smiled when he talked about his brother, and when Jackson smiled, he looked much younger. "You're not eighteen, are you?" Johnny blurted out.

Jackson blinked, but his smile remained. He reached down and pulled a slip of paper out of his shoe. It had the number *18* written on it.

"I stick this in my shoe, see," he said. "When the officers ask, *Are you over eighteen?* I say, *Yessir, I am. I am over eighteen.*"

Jackson and Johnny shared a laugh.

Johnny craned his sore neck and looked up at the starry sky. "Well, I'm glad you're here. And I bet that brother of yours is, too."

Jackson nodded so fast, Johnny could tell he was holding back tears. "I know he'd be proud of me, fighting for the Union. And I know I'll see him again. I know I'll see my brother again."

Johnny felt a pang in his heart.

Jackson sounded so sure.

Johnny hoped he'd see Louis and Lizzie again, too.

CHAPTER 8

Winter slowly thawed into spring, and 1861 slowly thawed into 1862. One day in early March, Captain McDougal ordered Johnny to play the General. It was the Break Camp Call, and it was the first call he'd ever played that sent up a giant *hurrah!* from the fellas.

The troops were leaving Covington! At long last!

"Strike the tents, boys!" the captain ordered. "Rip down those shelters and load up the wagons with as much wood as we can carry!"

That part didn't make sense to Johnny. Wouldn't there be wood where they were going?

They packed up the horses and filled canteens with

water. When it came time to douse the fire, Johnny dumped a bucket over a nearby flame, the first time the fire had been fully extinguished since the troops had arrived.

"You idiot!" William hissed, and pointed at the big plume of smoke Johnny caused. "You're sending up smoke signals to the rebels that we're on the move!"

Then it was Johnny's turn to pack. He rolled up his tin cup, plate, utensils, and sleeping pallet in his knapsack. He looked twice at the playing cards Harry had given him for his tenth birthday a few months ago and sheepishly decided to "forget" them. Heaven forbid he should get killed and word get back to Pop that he had those devil's playthings on his person. Nope, Johnny didn't want to be remembered as a gambler. Even if he only played for brass buttons.

Johnny covered the knapsack with leather to protect it from the rain. He slung it across his shoulder along with his canteen and strapped on his drum and sticks. It was everything Johnny owned, and he carried it all with pride.

As he scanned the frenzy of soldiers taking down tents and packing up valuables like chess sets and books and writing paper, a thought turned Johnny's stomach:

Would they be getting on a train?

———⊰⊙⊱———

"Johnny, sound the Quickstep," Captain McDougal ordered.

Johnny's stomach settled. The Quickstep was a marching call. They'd be walking out of Covington, Kentucky, not riding on one of those monstrous machines.

RrrrrraTAtat, rrrrraTAtat, rrrrratatatatataTAtatat.

It was a jaunty call, 110 beats per minute.

And WOW!

Johnny's drum moved an entire sea of soldiers forward, *BOOM BOOM BOOM.* The ground trembled under the pounding of thousands of feet. It was thunderous and powerful, and it all started with *him!*

"Git, now," William said, about a half mile down the way from camp. He glared at Reb, who bounded beside him, tongue and tail wagging. "Go on, you mutt!" William stamped his foot at Reb. Reb looked up at him with loyal eyes.

"Looks like he's coming with us," Johnny shouted over his drumroll.

William glared at him. Johnny smiled.

They'd only marched a mile or two outside of camp when Johnny realized how slow-going the progress would be. This many feet and hooves and wheels turned a muddy spring road to thick, gluey mush. The horses and wagons and cannons had to be pried from the muck every half mile or so. All the wood the captain made the troops bring suddenly made sense; they used most of it right away, as makeshift bridges over huge mud holes.

"No way we'll make our fifteen miles today," Harry muttered to Johnny. "I bet we make a dozen at best."

Even so, that evening, Johnny's feet were worn raw when the captain had him finally, *finally* drum Halt. Marching through mud made for huge, dirty blisters. Johnny peeled off wet socks that night, cringing in pain.

Jackson marched in a few minutes behind Johnny, barefoot. Jackson didn't have a proper uniform yet; the fellas hadn't scurried to find one for him, like they had for Johnny. Jackson looked cold and blistered, too, but he didn't complain once.

"Set up your bunks here," Captain McDougal said,

waving his hand over a field of green grass. "We set out again at six a.m."

The "bunks" were in bivouac—on the cold, wet ground, covered with a blanket. Johnny was so tired, he laid his head on his knapsack and fell fast asleep.

———◦◦◦◦———

Johnny woke the next morning stiff but well-rested. Putting his shoes back on his swollen, blistered feet was about the most painful thing he'd ever done in his life. Many of the fellas decided to march barefoot instead. After marching over their bloody footprints later that day, Johnny decided to stick with the shoes no matter what.

And so it went for the next twenty-five days.

They'd march a dozen-plus miles, then sleep on the ground.

They'd eat a little and complain a lot.

They'd say they couldn't walk another step, and then they'd walk another mile.

Crossing rivers was the worst. The troops would disassemble the Napoleons—the Union's heavy iron cannons—and float them across on pontoon boats made on-site. Depending on the current of the river, the

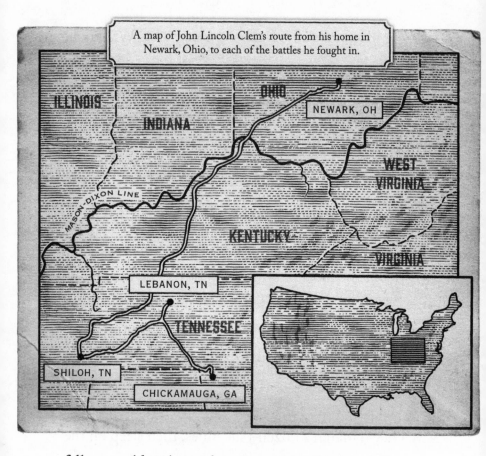

A map of John Lincoln Clem's route from his home in Newark, Ohio, to each of the battles he fought in.

fellas would either ride across on rafts themselves, or swim. Johnny hated swimming because his uniform stayed wet for hours after, and it chafed in unmentionable places when he marched. But at least he didn't have to swim holding a musket over his head, like many of the other fellas had to.

The troops lost two or three horses each time they crossed a river. Sometimes the horses were carrying food. Johnny missed every horse lost, but he missed the ones that carried food a little more.

When the troops entered Tennessee, the roads dried out. That seemed like a good thing, until the dust kicked up.

"Ack!" Johnny gagged. His eyes stung and watered. He could barely see the guy in front of him.

"Harry?" Johnny choked out. His teeth had a coating of grit, which tasted like mud.

"Yeah."

"Remind me to never complain about brushing my teeth ever again."

Harry gargled a laugh.

The troops were asleep on the ground one night in Tennessee in early April 1862 when Captain McDougal woke Johnny with the toe of his boot.

"Johnny," he said. He didn't whisper folks awake politely. "Sound a Salute."

Johnny scrambled to his feet, grabbed his drum, and played a series of three ruffles. The soldiers sleeping around him dragged themselves to standing.

A man on horseback galloped up, and Johnny swore the fella hopped off that horse before it came to a complete stop.

His uniform was that of a general. He wore an expression as if he had decided to drive his head through a brick wall and was about to do it.

"Men!" he barked into the starry night. "I'm General Grant. Welcome to Shiloh."

A portrait of Ulysses S. Grant on horseback, possibly during the Battle of Shiloh. *[LC-DIG-pga-02645]*

CHAPTER 9

After General Ulysses S. Grant's middle-of-the-night arrival, Johnny and the others did manage to go back to sleep, only to wake an hour or so later when the ground trembled and quaked. Dirt and rocks rained down on the Union troops as they scrambled out of sleep.

Confederate fire!

The men grabbed muskets and left valuable knapsacks behind.

"Who is the orderly drummer?" General Grant's voice thundered through camp. "I need the head drummer *now!*"

Johnny and the others swapped who was head drummer each week. This week, it was Johnny.

The air crackled with light and noise.

Jackson peered at Johnny with sleepy eyes. "You want me to go?"

Johnny swallowed and quickly counted to thirteen. "Nope. I—I'll be okay." His voice wasn't as strong as he wanted it to be, though.

William's mouth puckered. "You better be."

Johnny scrambled to General Grant's side and saluted. "Your orderly drummer reporting, *sir*!"

General Grant looked down at the drummer boy from his tall horse. His eyes narrowed, and Johnny could plainly see the general was wondering about his size, his age.

"You going to be able to serve your country, son? It's going to be dangerous."

Johnny thought of President Lincoln, urging folks to preserve the Union. He thought of Pop back home, and how all Pop wanted was to work on the railways and farm a plot of land in peace. He thought of Louis and Lizzie, and how he wanted to make them proud. He thought of Mom and angels instead of train wheels.

"Yes, sir!"

The general looked at his pocket watch. "Start the Long Roll at four forty-five a.m.—that's in five minutes. Play it without ceasing. Do you understand?"

Johnny nodded once. "Yes, sir!"

Play the Long Roll without stopping? It was a very aggressive call, a nonstop call to battle. It was usually only played for sixteen beats before another call sounded. Playing it nonstop meant the Union troops would charge against the enemy without pausing, without stopping to regroup. It meant a lot of lives would be lost.

A spray of light flared above. The ground shook. Showers of dirt flew over Johnny and the others.

———————◦◦◦◦———————

Johnny secured a white band around his left arm, showing the enemy that he was unarmed. The next five minutes passed like molasses and only served to make Johnny's stomach sicker and sicker. The thick, sweet smell of gunpowder smoke didn't help.

Four minutes.

Would Johnny fail his troops again?

Musket fire crackled and popped all around him, deadly bullets whizzed by.

Three minutes.

The night lit up with cannon fire. The earth erupted to Johnny's left.

Two minutes.

Johnny counted to thirteen, thirteen times.

Bullets whistled through the air, seeking Union flesh.

One minute.

Johnny's heart raced like a drum.

A drum.

He picked up his sticks. They felt like a part of his hands, his arms.

He ran his fingers over the snares of his drum. They felt like his muscles, holding his bones together.

Johnny swallowed and pushed aside the need to count to thirteen again.

The general gave him a signal. It was time.

He inhaled smoke and dirt and started playing the Long Roll: *prrrrt-trp-trp-tippy-tippy-trp-trp, prrrrt-trp-trp-tippy-tippy-trp-trp.*

"*Charrrrrge!*" Harry and the other fellas from the

Third Ohio scrambled up a hazy green hill toward a small log church.

Johnny kept playing. The boys to his left placed a fuse inside a cannon.

BOOM!

The earth shifted under Johnny's feet. The blast was so loud, he lost his hearing. But he kept playing based on the feel of his drum: *prrrrt-trp-trp-tippy-tippy-trp-trp, prrrrt-trp-trp-tippy-tippy-trp-trp.*

Wave after wave of Union soldiers charged up the hill, many of them falling to their knees or pushed backward by gunfire.

Shells sizzled and boomed over the rising sun.

The Confederate fire was getting closer. Shells and bullets and the grape—the hundreds of bits of lead that made up rebel cannon fire—tore up the ground and splintered trees all around Johnny. Rocks and dirt and smoke blinded him. But he kept playing: *prrrrt-trp-trp-tippy-tippy-trp-trp, prrrrt-trp-trp-tippy-tippy-trp-trp.*

The boys to Johnny's left wiped down the inside of the cannon with a wet sponge to fire it again. They were powerful beasts, the cannons. But watching those blue Union uniforms charge up the hill at the sound of his drum, Johnny realized his drum was a powerful beast, too.

His drum was a weapon. If you asked Johnny, it was the most powerful weapon on the battlefield. The loudest, too. His drum could be heard above the cannon fire. *Taptaptap*, his drum moved the troops forward. *Tappitytappitytappity*, they knew to retreat. He commanded the whole battlefield—every single Union soldier out there—with his two drumsticks.

Johnny stood taller. The Long Roll echoed louder.

A depiction of the Battle of Shiloh, fought on April 6 and 7, 1862. A roadway separates the Union forces on the right from the Confederate forces on the left. *[LC-DIG-pga-00540]*

General Grant galloped by, swinging a long, curved sword. "Nice work, soldier!" he yelled at Johnny. He rode off into the smoke.

Johnny's hands blistered, his shoulders burned, and his eyes stung and watered from smoke and dirt. His ears rang and made him dizzy. He was hungry and thirsty and tired and still wet from sleeping on the cold spring ground.

He kept playing.

After heaven knows how long, a fragment from an exploding shell silenced Johnny's drumbeats. The fragment would've hit his gut if it hadn't been for his drum.

Jackson stepped right up and took over the Long Roll while Johnny retreated. Johnny went to the back of the line, found a canteen someone had abandoned, and guzzled water to quench the fire in his throat. Once he had enough to drink, he'd head back out to the battlefield and help move the wounded and dead, like off-duty drummers were expected to do.

It was less smoky back there, behind the fire. Johnny could see a good ten or fifteen feet away, which is how he saw it all.

Harry.

Harry *ran*.

He didn't *limp* or *struggle.*

Any soldier back that far should be limping or struggling, because the only reason he should be behind the fighting was if he'd been hurt.

But Harry wasn't hurt.

And he didn't stop running.

He ran into the woods and disappeared.

Harry deserted the army.

Harry was a coward.

———✦———

All day, all night, and far into the next day, the Battle of Shiloh continued.

At long last, General Grant asked Jackson, who was back on duty after all the drummers had rotated through a shift, to sound the Retreat.

It took hours for the smoke to rise from the cold, wet ground.

When it finally did, Johnny had never seen an uglier sight.

CHAPTER 10

The smoke lifted off Shiloh like spirits leaving bodies. And oh! The mounds of bodies that cruel haze left behind! Thousands and thousands and thousands of them. Some soldiers had fought a terrible struggle with the monster death. Their faces warped with suffering, their dull eyeballs glared wide. Their hands were often full of the mud and grass they clutched in their last agony.

But the fellas who were still alive were worse. They moaned and howled like wild animals, dragging themselves and their bloody, twisted-torn bodies through the mud.

The medics trudged back and forth with their

Wounded Union soldiers receiving care in the aftermath of a battle.
[LC-DIG-stereo-1s02416]

stretchers, weary from hours of hauling boys to the sidelines. When they could use wagons, they did, but the ground was so torn up that the injured soldiers inside would scream in agony over every ditch and rut.

The earth was scorched and steaming. Deep, muddy

trenches scarred the land. Uprooted trees and bushes were scattered everywhere. Everything smelled like old gray smoke.

Captain McDougal sank to his knees and wept.

Johnny was so numb he could only stand nearby, arms hanging like lead at his sides. Tears streamed down his cheeks. He only knew that because he tasted them and the snot that poured from his nose. He couldn't breathe.

He couldn't breathe.

General Grant closed his eyes and bowed his head. Then he snapped to attention. "Johnny," he said. "Drum the Surgeon's Call again by that tent so the boys can find their way to the hospital."

Johnny retrieved a new, undamaged drum and sounded the call. Several of the moaning, howling, injured boys limped toward him.

"Good work," General Grant said. He placed his hands on Johnny's shoulders. "Not all of them can make it to the infirmary, though. I need you and the other drummers to go out there"—he pointed his thumb at the black ground scattered with bodies—"and find the boys who are still alive."

Johnny nodded. He had done this during the battle

itself. But doing this in the deep stillness that came after the cannons and guns quieted felt eerie and shameful, like walking on graves.

Johnny tiptoed over gnarled, stiffened bodies; those poor fellas were long gone. "Help, anyone?" he whispered. It sounded like he was screaming.

Step.

"Anyone need help?"

Step.

"Hello?"

A hand reached out and snagged Johnny's ankle.

He gasped.

"Water," said the voice below.

Johnny crouched next to the fella. His left leg had splintered apart like driftwood. He was covered in blood.

Johnny scrambled to unscrew the top off his canteen. He poured water down the soldier's throat. The fella gargled as he drank it.

"Over here!" Johnny yelled to the medics across the field. "Here!"

The medics gave him a halfhearted wave. They already had someone on their stretcher.

This fella's lips were blackened from ripping open gunpowder pouches with his teeth, so Johnny knew he was infantry. He poured water on the soldier's face and swiped at it with a corner of his shirt.

"We'll just clean you up," Johnny said, his voice shaky. "That help?"

The man nodded, tried to smile. His head lolled back.

"Stay with me, okay?" Johnny said. He heard the desperation in his voice and hoped this fella didn't. "They'll be here in a minute."

"Thank you."

Then the light in his eyes went out.

His body went slack.

Johnny had *known* death before. But he'd never *seen* death before. Not right next to him.

A shadow fell over Johnny and the soldier. Johnny looked up at a medic. "He didn't make it," he said. "This one didn't make it."

The medic pushed up his tiny wire glasses on his nose. "This one and thousands more."

———◆◆◆———

The Union troops stayed near Shiloh for a handful of days, licking their wounds.

On the battlefield, dead artillery horses and their dead riders were piled in heaps. Flies swarmed everywhere. The warm spring sun caused a stench that was almost unbearable. Johnny vomited more than once, usually when he saw a limb with no body.

The troops dug trenches and rolled the dead into them. They covered the bodies with three or four inches of dirt. It was as proper a burial as the soldiers could give their fallen friends. Jackson said a quick prayer over each body. Each and every one. Some of the fellas told him to get a move on, but he kept praying.

"These graves'll be washed away by the first rain," Jackson muttered, looking at the mounds the troops were leaving behind. Johnny imagined the locals having to deal with the buzzards and crows and other creatures that would swarm later, picking at the flesh and leaving the bones.

In the infirmary, some of the soldiers still hadn't

been treated three days later. The boys in there burned with high fevers, and their wounds swelled red and filled with pus. They tried to forget their pain by comparing their injuries.

"A minié ball shattered this here bone—see? Snapped it clean in two."

"You think your little scrape looks bad? Cannon shell, right here. Ripped the skin right off my buttock. I'll never sit again!"

Most of them couldn't joke, though. There was very little water, and the water the troops did find in nearby streams smelled like corpses. Soldiers died of thirst. Johnny promised never to curse the rain again.

The medics never slept. They merely wiped off their bloody instruments on their aprons and moved to the next patient. They collapsed a lot, too.

But Johnny and the others got word that the Union had won this battle.

Winning didn't feel as glorious as Johnny had thought it would.

CHAPTER 11

"**K**eep marching, boys!" Captain McDougal yelled down at the troops from his high horse. "Only ten days till we make Nashville. Nine if we double-time it!"

"Easy for him to say," Johnny muttered to Jackson. "Ten days on a horse doesn't compare to ten days of walking."

Jackson nodded. He was the quiet type. The Union troops had left Shiloh two days before, and Jackson had said maybe three sentences the whole time.

On walks like these, Johnny sure did miss Harry and his nonstop jokes. But thinking of that guy made Johnny angry all over again. Harry's buddies mourned him, thinking he was one of the dead guys who'd been blasted apart so badly no one could recognize him. Johnny knew better, of course. But he thought it was best that Harry's buddies considered him a hero instead of the coward he really was. Sometimes Johnny wondered if he should tell them the truth.

On the third day of walking, the late-April weather was cool and dry, so the captain made the fellas go twenty-two miles. Twenty-two. Johnny's feet swelled so much that he had to ditch his old, small shoes. They were barely hanging on to his feet anyway. He tore up his shirt and wrapped it around his feet. It didn't help.

Johnny was thirsty and sunburned and dirty. And hungry. Boy, was he hungry. He was so tired of eating hardtack. But still he pulled one out of his knapsack and gnawed on it.

"If I see a hardtack biscuit in heaven, I might tell old Saint Peter himself to go boil his shirt," Johnny said. The boys marching nearby got a laugh out of that.

Johnny's pay sat in his pocket, but out here in nowhere, it was useless. He couldn't spend Union dollars in the Confederacy. Not easily. Not *safely*. He could eat it to pad his belly—that might be useful.

William's dog, Reb, who still marched loyally beside the troops, stopped. He arched his back and growled.

The blue sky fizzed and exploded.

Confederate fire!

Johnny dropped into a roadside ditch along with several others. William drummed off a rapid Alarm Call, based on orders from Captain McDougal. The Union boys loaded muskets and fired back.

It was a quick skirmish, especially when the Confederates who fired on the troops realized it was a whole regiment, not just a handful of guys. The rebels threw down their muskets and sabers and jumped off their horses. Surrender!

The Union troops rounded up the prisoners, tying their wrists and ankles with thick rope.

Just as the troops were about to leave, Johnny noticed a rebel lying in tall weeds. A fella about his age. A little older, a little bigger.

Dead.

His blood soaked into the dirt around him.

This one, because he was so close to Johnny's age, made Johnny's throat squeeze shut.

Johnny reached down and gently closed the rebel's eyes.

And then he took the dead boy's boots.

They were too big. But those worthless dollars in Johnny's pocket finally went to good use, padding the toes of his new shoes.

"Almost to Nashville, boys," one of the fellas muttered. The Third Ohio had been walking for eight days. Johnny closed his eyes and still marched in time. If a person could walk and sleep at the same time, the Third Ohio knew how.

The closer they got to Nashville, the more farms cropped up. Johnny thought of Pop, and how he'd be prepping the fields for corn now, since it was almost May.

Corn.

His stomach grumbled.

Johnny could eat a whole cob right now. Straight off the plant, no cooking or nothing.

The troops passed a small gray house with a small gray man rocking on the front porch. Captain McDougal tipped his hat at him and galloped ahead.

"Don't you go howdying me, you Union scum!" the

old man shouted into the cloud of dust the captain had kicked up. "You listen here!"

One of the Union soldiers laughed and saluted him.

The man grumbled, stooped, and stood up with a shotgun.

He fired.

He missed every last fella.

But boy, did his fire ignite something.

The Union boys fell out of line, twenty or thirty total. They screamed and yelled and hurrahed, hopping over his white picket fence. Before Johnny knew it, he found himself barging through the old man's front door and being pushed into the kitchen.

"The cellar!" someone yelled.

"Over here!"

"Oh, law! He has a smokehouse, too!"

This old man's home was filled to the brim with bacon and ham and vegetables and preserves and, and . . .

When a guy is as hungry as the Third Ohio fellas were, he doesn't think. He *takes*.

And when he's as hungry as the Third Ohio fellas were, and he eats a real meal for the first time in weeks, he eats until he makes himself sick. Sick and vomiting.

The Union boys tore apart that house and left the contents of their sick bellies behind.

"C'mon," someone groaned. "We gotta go before the captain finds us here."

"We punished that old slave owner just half enough," said one of the Union fellas, laughing his way out the front door. The soldier who had leveled his musket at the rebel while his buddies raided the old man's home lowered it at last.

As Johnny hauled his sick self back over the fence, he heard crying. He stopped.

The old man still sat in his rocker. He was bawling.

"I don't own no slaves," he cried. "Don't nobody I know own slaves. I'm just protecting my farm. I'm here by my lonesome. My boys are at war. And now thanks to y'all, I got nothing. Nothing!"

He looked so much like Johnny's pop, sitting there.

This is everybody's war, Johnny thought. *Not just soldiers'.*

CHAPTER 12

The Third Ohio made camp in Lebanon, outside of Nashville, Tennessee. It was now full-on summer, and their blue wool uniforms stank with sweat. The troops pitched limp canvas tents, using bayonets for tent pegs and candleholders. The fellas settled in under thick, cool, peppery-smelling cedar trees.

Under those tall, shady trees, the troops were well-hidden from Confederate attackers. But the vermin attackers found them, all right.

Lice.

Those nasty little gray bugs struck with the force of an insect army. They got into *everything*: the bunks, the clothes, the hair, the eyebrows, the parts unmentionable.

They laid eggs like mad and made the fellas scratch their skin to shreds. The soldiers didn't have razors to shave themselves bald. They couldn't beat 'em.

To distract themselves, and because most of the boys, like Johnny, had left their playing cards in other campsites, they found a new way to win money off others. They'd lay out a tin plate, pick a louse bug off, and bet on whose insect could scurry the fastest across the plate.

"Go, Tiny!"

"C'mon, Grayback! Run, you dummy!"

"Woo-hoo! Did you see how fast my Nasty was? That bug is a true champ."

A soldiers' camp from 1864. [LC-DIG-ppmsca-33099]

Johnny won three whole dollars with his louse, General Lee.

Other critters found the boys, too. Worms and weevils wiggled their way into the hardtack supply. The good news was they were easily skimmed off and didn't leave any distinct flavor behind. The bad news was sometimes a fella would get a biteful of worm with his cracker.

It was funny, too, calling those things *crackers,* 'cause they were more likely to crack a guy's teeth than his teeth were to crack them. Long about early June, Johnny bit into one and left half a front tooth behind.

"Hey, fellas!" He laughed, bucking his teeth at them. "Look! My first war wound!"

All the guys laughed at that. William laughed loudest of all.

Later that day, Johnny saw William hunched over a piece of paper. William wrote a letter home every chance he got; the others liked to call him "Mama's Boy" for it. But here, now, he wasn't writing. He was scratching at lice and muttering cuss words, twiddling his quill in his hand.

"Everything okay back home, William?" Johnny asked.

An envelope for a letter sent during the Civil War.
[LC-DIG-ppmsca-34643]

He startled. "Oh! Yeah. It's just that"—he cut his eyes left and right, to make sure no other fellas were near—"that money I lost in those lice bets? Now I don't have anything to send home, and, well . . ."

His voice dropped off, and he looked at the blank piece of paper, at the letter he couldn't write.

"And your mama needs the money, doesn't she?" Johnny asked. It all made sense now, why William cared more about his salary than preserving the Union. Why he was always such a model soldier. He *needed* this job; he didn't *want* it.

Johnny popped off his boot and fished the wad of bills out of the toe.

He offered it to William. "You can send her this."

William swatted his hand away. "We don't need your charity, and we certainly don't need your nasty shoe money!"

He stormed off.

Johnny looked at the blank piece of paper William left behind, at the quill and the ink made from pokeberry juice.

Maybe I should write home? Johnny thought.

Dear Pop, he wrote. The pen felt foreign in his hand. Not like a drumstick at all.

Johnny left that piece of paper sitting there, just like that.

Dear Pop.

The summer of 1862, drought set in. Drought does three things:

1. It kills all the crops.
2. It dries up all the springs.
3. It makes hungry, thirsty soldiers do stupid things.

The springs the troops camped next to had long since dried up, and the deer and rabbits that the fellas would sometimes trap were smart enough to move on. But the Third Ohio hadn't received its next orders yet, so it wasn't able to move on.

Once, after a brief flash thunderstorm, the boys ran into the rain with tongues sticking out, cups extended to catch the precious drops. After the clouds parted, the fellas took their tin spoons and dipped them into mud puddles. In a moment of cleverness, they decided to strain it through their sweaty, dirty handkerchiefs first.

Then—yep.

Johnny and the others drank it.

Muddy water tasted exactly like muddy water.

And it passed right through a person like muddy water.

About a half day after Johnny drank from the mud puddle, his stomach cramped like a fist punching him from the inside. He couldn't stand straight, let alone make it to the outhouse trenches in time.

It was *awful*.

The smell, the cramping, the fever, the shakes.

And almost every fella in camp caught it.

"Dysentery," the medic told Johnny. The doc pushed up those wire spectacles of his on his long nose. "And it'll get worse before it gets better."

The smell of diarrhea hung over camp like a green cloud, while ninety-nine fellas out of a hundred shivered and cramped underneath it.

"Drink this," the medic said. Johnny choked down a mixture of whiskey and blackberry juice. It didn't stay with him long. The doc rubbed alcohol on Johnny's chest and made him wear every layer of clothing he owned, even though it was summer and the clothes were covered in lice. Johnny shivered and shook under the thick pile, his tongue as dry and fat as a wad of cotton.

Oh, he wanted water!

He wanted water so badly, that at one point, he tapped on his nearby drum with his fingers: the Water Call. The other thirsty, feverish boys in the sick tent laughed.

William was sick, too, but he refused to see the doctors. "Those quacks don't know a thing! Nope," he'd say, then bend in half with a stomach cramp. "I'll do fine on my own, thanks."

Johnny wondered if William was right, because as

each day passed, another one of the fellas would pass with it.

Dead.

And not on a battlefield.

Dead from no water.

Dead from the contents of his stomach not staying put.

Dead far from home, far from glory.

It seemed like the worst, most cruel death of all.

CHAPTER 13

The fellas recovered from the bout of dysentery after two or three weeks. "Hang in there until the next big rain," Doc said. "You'll be all right once it rains." It was the truth; once the boys had enough fresh drinking water to flush their systems, most everyone improved back to 100 percent. Some fellas swore, though, that their stomachs were never the same again.

The Third Ohio lost more boys to sickness than to bullets.

The regiment stayed under those tall, earthy cedar trees through the summer, while other regiments moved throughout the South. The Third Ohio moved here and there when it was needed in a fight, but it would move back to Lebanon afterward. It became "home."

"Welcome to Tennessee, boys!" Johnny said to other troops who camped with them for a night or two before marching on. "Home of pretty girls and ugly dogs, according to the locals." That always got a laugh. "We don't have any pretty girls, but we've got us an ugly dog!" Johnny pointed to William's dog, Reb, who would wag his tail, agreeing with his ugliness. The fellas howled.

Union soldiers posing by the company kitchen. These log cookeries were typical of Civil War camps. *[LC-USZC6-46]*

Dang, that dog was cute. Johnny scratched him and thanked him for being the butt of his jokes.

"Hey, I heard of you!" sometimes a fella from another troop would say to Johnny. "You're that kid Grant praised at Shiloh!"

"Yeah, we heard about you, Johnny Shiloh!"

"What a kid!"

It made Johnny feel proud, until they got to the *what a kid* part. And they always got to the *what a kid* part.

When the green leaves turned gold, another troop marched through.

The Seventy-Ninth Colored.

Some of the men in the regiment were escaped slaves, like Jackson. Some of them were free when the war began. All of them were colored men. And there wasn't a regiment more proud to wear Union blue than those fellas.

Jackson never stopped talking, not the whole time, to those guys. "My brother, see. He's eight now? I haven't seen him in three years. He's in Alabama, last I heard. You from Alabama, too? What part? Oh, yeah, pretty falls near there. Chewacla, I think? Yeah, so, my brother, see . . ."

Two unidentified African American Union soldiers.
[LC-DIG-ppmsca-13484]

The next day, when the Seventy-Ninth moved out, Jackson decided to go with them.

Johnny shook his head when Jackson told him. "No," Johnny said. "You got a good job with us. You got friends here. Right?"

Jackson shrugged. "I got you."

Johnny realized then that no one else in the regiment had made Jackson feel at home. That he'd stuck with the Third Ohio all this time because of Johnny.

"But those guys"—Jackson tilted his head at the Seventy-Ninth, who were almost done breaking camp—"so many of them, they're looking for relatives, too, see. Those guys know what's important to me."

Johnny thought back to his argument with Pop, and how Pop didn't understand how badly Johnny needed to fight for the Union. He sighed.

Jackson offered his drumsticks to Johnny. Johnny had forgotten that he'd loaned them to him.

"But aren't you drumming for them?" Johnny asked, lifting his chin at Jackson's new regiment.

He nodded. "I guess I can find other sticks. I'd pay you for them, except . . ."

Except he didn't have any money. Jackson had been allowed to stay with the Third Ohio, but he hadn't received a salary like Johnny had. He'd been paid in food and shelter.

"Are you kidding? Take them."

Jackson twiddled the drumsticks between his fingers. "You mean that?"

"The Seventy-Ninth needs a drummer. Pretty useless drummer you'd be, without sticks." Johnny shoved him and smiled.

Jackson did the same to Johnny. "I'll pay you back someday. I promise."

When the Seventy-Ninth moved out, Jackson stood tall, wearing his drum and an ear-to-ear smile. He drummed a loud, proud Direct Step Call. The Seventy-Ninth marched.

One of the other fellas from the Third Ohio elbowed Johnny and mimicked his pout, teasing him for the sad look on his face.

"Tear in my eye?" Johnny whispered with a wink. "What tear in my eye?" But it was there.

Before Johnny knew it, William grabbed up his own drum and rattled off a Pioneer's Call.

A Pioneer's Call!

Most everyone in the Third Ohio gasped. The Pioneer's Call was a clean-the-camp call. Drumming it when someone left camp meant you were driving out scoundrels.

Johnny saw red. Before he could stop himself, he snatched William's drum from his grip and punched a hole clean through it.

William growled but was too much of a coward to do anything about it.

Jackson's eye twinkled back at Johnny. Johnny knew it was a silent *thanks*.

"Find your brother!" Johnny yelled after Jackson.

"I will, John Lincoln Clem! I will!"

CHAPTER 14

Slowly, 1862 passed into 1863. One of the boys of the Third Ohio, who was good at keeping up with such things, guessed they marched almost 1,500 miles that year. And now they were on the move again. At last.

Johnny drummed the General Call to signal it was time to break camp. The troops tore down all the wood shelters they'd built to survive the winter. They packed wagons and horses and met up with dozens of other regiments outside of Nashville.

"Next stop, Chickamauga!" Captain McDougal shouted.

The troops marched.

Johnny was lonelier than ever.

No Harry. No Jackson.

Sure, Johnny had other friends in the Third Ohio. But they treated him like the little drummer boy. "Johnny Shiloh" they called him, after General Grant said all those nice things about him in that battle. But Johnny wasn't a hero in their eyes. He was still a kid, even though now he was twelve.

The troops were only a few days outside of Lebanon, hiking through mountains so tall, the climb left the fellas dizzy and gasping, when the accident happened.

The horse and wagon carrying nearly all the food—bacon, hardtack, coffee, baked beans, rashers—toppled off a steep cliff in the Tennessee mountains.

Some of the boys tried to scramble down the cliff to save what they could. They climbed back up empty-handed.

"Food landed in a creek far below," one of them said. "Can't get to it, and even if we could, it'd be ruined."

Now they marched with growling bellies.

It was one thing to be tired and sore and marching. It was another to be tired and sore and hungry and marching.

Johnny's stomach yelled at him to find food. There wasn't any hunting because the stamping of thousands of marching feet made the wildlife scatter far from the path. Johnny grabbed bark off a pine tree and chewed on it. The inner bark was supposed to be sweet and juicy. It wasn't. It tasted like dirt. Horrible.

One morning, an Assembly Call sounded. Early, while everyone was still asleep. It was confusing because they didn't usually drum those kinds of calls on the march.

The boys rubbed the morning dew out of their eyes.

William loomed over the group, his repaired drum by his side. He bared his teeth.

"Who took him? Where is he?"

Johnny blinked. "Where is who?"

"Reb."

William's voice waivered when he said his dog's name. Johnny thought back to the last time he'd seen the mutt. It had been a day or so.

Johnny shook his head. "I don't know—"

"You hated that dog, Johnny. What did you do to him?"

"Now, you wait a second," Johnny said, hopping to his feet. "I loved that dog, too."

William swiped furiously at his eyes with the back of his hand. "If I find out you did anything to Reb—" William stopped talking and dragged his finger across his throat.

Johnny swallowed. He didn't doubt William would do it, neither.

William stormed away, and some of the fellas from a different regiment chuckled and elbowed each other.

Licked their lips.

Johnny's empty stomach lurched.

He guessed then what they'd done with Reb.

———◦◦◦———

Johnny felt sick for a long time after that, marching all through the next day. He didn't tell William what those fellas had done, because he wasn't a rat. He didn't have any proof, neither. But he felt pretty darn sure of it.

The night they reached the campsite near South Pittsburg, Tennessee, Johnny felt as blue as he had the whole time he'd been away from home.

Home.

Maybe it was time to go back.

He wasn't a "real" soldier, after all. He could leave and it wouldn't be dishonorable.

Except it *would* be dishonorable. To him.

Johnny still believed in restoring the Union.

He still believed in returning home a hero.

"Hey, Johnny Shiloh!" one of the fellas from the Third Ohio called out. "How's about you musicians play us a tune?"

Johnny almost shrugged them off but then thought, *Hey. A little music might help.* And he didn't want to ask William to play for these guys. Not today.

The fifer, the bugler, and Johnny played "Soldier's Joy," "Buffalo Gals," and "Swallow Tail Jig" as the fellas called out songs they wanted to hear. They sang along, loud and swaying, with their arms draped around one another's shoulders. Johnny's spirits started to lift, as they always did when he was drumming.

His heart and his drum beat the same rhythm.

"Johnny Shiloh!" one of the guys hollered. "Let's hear 'Just Before the Battle, Mother.'"

Hmmm.

Johnny hated that song.

"Nah . . ." he said.

"Yeah!" another fella yelled. "Let's hear it!"

The lyrics of that song went *Farewell, Mother. You may never press me to your heart again.*

Every time Johnny had to play that one, his mouth went bitter.

He didn't have a mother to sing to anymore.

"How about another one, fellas?"

"No," one of the Third Ohio guys grumbled. "We want *that* song. Don't be a whiny kid."

Johnny unstrapped his drum and set it on the ground.

And he walked away.

One of the boys of the Twenty-Second Michigan followed him.

"John," he said.

Johnny stopped.

"Name's George," the guy said. He had a mop of dirty red hair and was maybe nineteen. He extended his rough hand for a handshake. Johnny narrowed his eyes at the guy, like maybe he was teasing. Nobody shook hands with a kid. But the guy stuck his hand out farther, so Johnny shook it.

"Those guys back there," he said, pointing at the regiment Johnny had been with for the last two years. "They don't see it."

"See what?" Johnny asked.

"The fire. You got it, soldier."

Soldier!

"Come with us, soldier. Come to Chickamauga with the Twenty-Second. We plan on being heroes."

The next morning, when the Twenty-Second Michigan regiment broke camp early and headed out, Johnny left with them.

A few fellas of the Third Ohio tried to stop him.

"We've paid your salary!" they said.

"You're our good-luck charm!"

"Stay with us for Harry's sake!"

Johnny knew he'd be sad, leaving most of these fellas behind. Not William. But some of the others.

He looked at the drum, still lying in the grass where he'd laid it last night. He loved that drum. But that drum, it was safe. Sure, he might still get hurt being a drummer, but he wouldn't ever be a hero, either, pounding that thing. No, sometimes we have to give up the things that are safe and take a big risk. Like Jackson did, leaving with the Seventy-Ninth Colored.

"I have to go, fellas," Johnny said, hooking his knapsack over his shoulder. "Those guys know what's important to me."

CHAPTER 15

The Twenty-Second Michigan had about five hundred men, so Johnny became part of the pack easily. Finally, they stopped outside of Chickamauga, Georgia, just over the Tennessee line, and prepared for the battle ahead.

The soldiers received three days of rations. They filled their water canteens. And Johnny received his first musket! It was sawed off to allow for his height, and boy, was it a beauty! It was still heavy, but he'd built up strong muscles, thanks to hauling around his drum.

Ammunition was doled out, the weapons inspected. Those were the official duties of heading into battle.

The *unofficial* duties of heading into battle included

writing your name and address on a small slip of paper. The soldiers pinned these inside their uniforms in case their bodies needed to be identified. *John Lincoln Clem, Newark, Ohio.* Pop and Louis and Lizzie had never felt so far away as they did while Johnny wrote that.

Unofficial duties also included pelting one another with rotten green apples to burn off nerves.

And then, they waited.

Dang, that part was hard. Every snapped twig, every crunched leaf made a fella jump when he knew what he was headed into.

And there were lots of twigs and leaves, all right. This part of the country sure was beautiful: tall trees, rolling green mountains. But the land made it hard to know where the enemy was. The Union lifted a man above the treetops in a gas-filled balloon, tethered to the ground, to spot the rebels' formations. Union General Rosecrans stood below, translating the hand signals from the man in the balloon.

"My drummer!" the general yelled after he had the information he needed. "I need my drummer NOW!"

There was a drum sitting nearby, but no boy with a white armband tied around his arm, signaling his status. Johnny gulped.

He could drum out those orders. But wouldn't that be taking a step backward? He wanted to do big things! Heroic things!

"I need to relay these orders! WHERE IS MY DRUMMER?"

Johnny stepped forward and laid down his musket. He snatched up the drum and saluted.

"What are they, sir?"

The general barked a few commands: the Assemble, the Advance, the Left Wheel. Johnny played them flawlessly on someone else's drum.

The troops moved. Johnny wanted so badly to move with them, but he held that drum.

The general looked at the drum, not even adjusted to Johnny's size, and then looked at his sawed-off musket lying in the grass.

"You a soldier or a drummer, son?" General Rosecrans asked.

Johnny didn't pause. "Both, sir!"

"Why do you want to be a soldier? You're a fine drummer."

An illustration of John Lincoln Clem holding a rifle, as he would have looked after his commission as a sergeant. *[LC-DIG-ds-00297]*

The troops were still moving forward, leaving Johnny behind. "I don't like to be shot at without shooting back, sir!"

The general's face twitched. He placed both hands on Johnny's shoulders. "Son, I gotta make this fast. But you did fine work today. I'm commissioning you as a sergeant for the Twenty-Second Michigan in the United States Army."

Wow!

A real live soldier with a rank!

Of . . . sergeant.

Johnny barely remembered to salute General Rosecrans before he said, "General, is that all you're going to make me?"

The other drummer boy returned and took a harsh cussing from the general for picking *that exact* moment to go into the woods to relieve himself. Johnny double-timed his march and caught up with the Twenty-Second Michigan. His heart pounded.

The drumrolls behind him told him where to go. Johnny knew with all his heart that the drum wouldn't let him down.

And now he understood how those other fellas felt, hearing his drum. There was so much marching, moving, aligning, *waiting* before the actual fighting began. Hearing the drum ended the suspense.

The drum steered the troops left. Johnny's heart pounded out the call.

The cool air sizzled and crackled.

The first Confederate fire!

"IIIiiiiiiEEEEeeee! IIiiiiEEEeeee!" Hordes of men in gray uniforms charged at the Union troops, screeching the famous rebel yell.

Johnny dove behind a tree.

Snap!

A branch cracked beside him.

He whirled around the tree trunk, musket raised to his shoulder.

Union blue!

He swallowed, ducked back behind the tree.

Heavens! he thought. *Help me shoot the right guys!*

The drum told Johnny to advance farther.

A thunderous cannon boomed, rattling Johnny to his core.

Dirt and debris dusted his eyes.

He advanced.

Bullets whizzed and whistled, flying by Johnny like deadly ghosts.

A man nearby dropped to his knees.

Johnny suddenly felt stronger than he had in a month.

The booming and whirring, moaning and screeching became one large battlefield *hum.*

Johnny scrambled through stinging, choking smoke and thick, gnarly brush. He thought about the boys who didn't have shoes anymore, tearing through these thorns and briars barefoot, and wished them luck.

He found one of the deep trenches some of the other Union boys had dug. He hopped down into it. A wooden barricade in front of the trench took most of the fire, but that meant shards of wood rained down on the soldiers inside. Sometimes huge logs fell with a crash.

Johnny's musket had one round in it, but he was too short to aim the barrel up and out of this deep trench. One of the other soldiers must've seen him trying, though, because the fella kicked a wooden box. "Here!" he shouted louder than the bullets whizzing overhead. "Stand on this!"

It was a wooden box of powder cartridges. Johnny scrambled on top of it.

Perfect!

"Just pray that box don't get hit while you're standing on it!" The soldier leaned in close to Johnny's ear. "You'll be blown to high heaven if a bullet finds that box!"

Johnny gulped, aimed his musket over the rim of the trench, and fired.

He hit nothing.

A bullet hit something nearby with a sickening crack. Johnny thought it was the log above him until he saw the fella who had pointed out the box grab his arm and howl in pain.

His bone. The bullet had cracked against the fella's bone.

Johnny started reloading.

Nine steps for a reload. Johnny tore open a powder cartridge with his teeth. Some of the gritty black powder got on his lips. It tasted like solid smoke.

Then he dumped the powder and the bullet into the shaft. His hands shook.

Cannon fire hit somewhere so close by, Johnny stumbled.

He almost spilled the contents of the cartridge on the ground. He'd seen other fellas reload hundreds of times, but doing this here, with bullets flying around, sure made his nerves jump.

He packed the powder down with a ramrod.

He cocked and fired again.

Again, he hit nothing.

This went on for hours. Johnny was so tired, he saw double. So when he watched the Twenty-Second

Michigan's battle flag fall to the ground, he doubted what he saw.

Before he even thought about it, Johnny scrambled out of the trench.

"Don't do that!" one of the fellas yelled. "Someone will pick it up!"

But this was his regiment, the one that believed in him enough to make him a sergeant. He wasn't about to let his colors, with its proud eagle and its three shining stars, lie in the dirt.

But before he got to it, a Confederate grabbed it and ran.

Johnny watched that rebel dash through the forest waving *his* colors and screeching that horrible rebel yell.

It felt like a mighty big loss for the Union boys.

A shrill whistle grew closer, louder.

Johnny's hat flew off his head.

He scrambled to pick it up and place it back on his noggin. He wasn't going to be a sergeant without a full uniform, no, sir.

When he got back to the trench, the other fellas' eyes widened.

"You sure got lucky out there," one of them said, pointing at Johnny's hat.

Three minié balls had blazed right through the felt of his cap. Right next to his scalp!

Johnny vomited.

At sunset, the Union soldiers heard the drummer call Retreat.

Retreat. It sounded a lot like *defeat*.

The soldiers turned north, toward Chattanooga.

The Twenty-Second Michigan was down from 500 men to about 250.

As the sun set and the stars rose, Johnny laid out his pallet on the ground.

General Rosecrans paced and cracked his knuckles. "Long day, boys. Long, hard day. Tomorrow will be better."

Tomorrow.

Johnny had barely finished thinking the word when he lay down on top of his gun, placed his head on his metal canteen for a pillow, and fell asleep.

CHAPTER 16

Whistling and crackling explosions will yank a soldier from his slumber.

Johnny woke this way, scrambling from sleep to Confederate cannon fire.

It was September 20, 1863, the second day of the Battle of Chickamauga.

Johnny snatched up his musket and considered leaving his knapsack and canteen behind. Every little thing a soldier *doesn't* bring into battle means he can run faster, dive quicker, sweat less.

But leaving his valuables behind felt like saying, *I may not need these things after today.* So Johnny quickly picked them up, bundled them together, and slung the pack over his shoulder.

Today, the Union troops marched farther south before heading into the fighting. If they could push the Confederate troops west, they'd win today. They needed a win today.

They hadn't won yesterday.

They hadn't won in a while.

The Union troops looped back to face north. Once in position, Johnny advanced when the drum told him to.

Deadly metal bits swarmed the air.

There weren't trenches that far south, so Johnny ducked behind trees and under bushes. Once, he wheeled around a small hill and came face-to-face with—

A cannon!

He almost lost the contents of his bowels.

But oh. Wait.

No.

It wasn't a cannon at all. It was a giant log, set up on old wagon wheels, made to look like a cannon. Johnny had heard of those rascally rebels setting up Quaker guns, fake cannons used to confuse the Union boys.

It worked.

The crackling of weapons grew louder.

Johnny ducked under the fake cannon and watched the enemy in gray approach.

He gulped. He was trapped! He wouldn't be able to reload his musket in this cramped space. He'd be captured under there for sure.

But most of them ran right by, their feet thundering.

They didn't even see him!

Johnny guessed being small could sometimes be a big advantage.

And then he saw an opportunity.

Most of the Confederates had run past, toward the fight going on behind him. In doing so, they'd left their colonel, a very decorated old soldier, sitting high on his horse.

Unprotected.

It wasn't good fighting etiquette, a sergeant like Johnny hiding and shooting a colonel like him off his mount. And Johnny wouldn't do it if it wasn't the way a hero would do it.

So he scooted on his belly out from under the cannon. He stood and aimed his sawed-off musket at him.

"Colonel, I demand your surrender."

The colonel turned and paused. Johnny could tell the rebel was trying to calculate his age. Johnny tried to control his shaking musket.

The colonel galloped over and drew his long silver sword from its holster. He laid the tip of the blade against Johnny's throat. Without thinking, Johnny lowered his musket.

"Me?" the colonel said. "I don't think so. Surrender, you dreadful little Yankee."

Johnny counted to thirteen, his lucky number.

After that, he thought of his mother.

He hadn't been her hero.

But he could be one now.

Johnny stooped as though he was laying down his weapon. But as he did, he quietly cocked the hammer and swung his hand down the barrel.

Johnny lifted his musket.

He shot.

He hit the colonel in his right thigh.

The colonel fell off his horse with a bone-cracking sound.

Blood spurted everywhere.

Johnny felt sick.

The horse galloped away.

The colonel clutched his leg and howled.

Johnny swallowed and leaned over the colonel.

The wound was bad, but not bad enough to kill him.

Should he shoot again?

No. Heroes don't shoot a man on the ground.

Johnny waited with him. Hearing this old fella moan and cuss, Johnny didn't feel very heroic. He stayed until he saw the Union medics with their white armbands, and he flagged them over.

"Take this colonel prisoner," Johnny said. "I'm heading back into battle."

The heavy roll of musketry and the terrible thunder of artillery continued throughout the day. It was chilly, and the cool earth and thick trees held the smoke close to the ground. It was hard to breathe, hard to see.

Johnny followed the orders of the drum and wheeled to his right. The battle grew thicker, closer, and soon the fighting took place face-to-face. Blue and gray uniforms clashed, using bayonets, fists, feet, teeth, stones, sticks, fence posts—anything they could get their hands on. Johnny trudged over a hill and toward a small clearing, only to see fifty or so gray uniforms charging his way.

There was nowhere to hide. And Johnny was clever

A depiction of the Battle of Chickamauga, fought on September 19 and 20, 1863. *[LC-DIG-pga-01846]*

enough to know that while he might be able to fight one man, maybe two, there was no way a twelve-year-old soldier like him could handle fighting several nineteen- and twenty-year-old men.

And the Union boys were outnumbered.

So he did the only thing he could think to do: he clutched his gut like he'd been shot, dropped to the ground, and played dead, just like Reb used to do. He clutched handfuls of grass and mud and lay as still as a rock.

"IIIIiiiiEEEEEeeee!"

Those rebels screeched and screamed all around, but they left Johnny lying there.

Bullets and cannon fire pummeled into the ground all around him, and yet Johnny lay perfectly still. It was far easier to get shot, just lying there.

"Hurrah!"

Hundreds of feet sounded behind him, and Johnny saw, because he was smart enough to "die" with his eyes open, that more Union boys were headed his way.

Fighting broke out all around him.

Teeth and blood and cuss words flew.

Johnny lay there.

Watching.

He wanted to cry at the things he saw, but dead boys don't cry.

Faces twisted in anger.

Bodies twisted in pain.

Ugly, horrible stuff, war.

After what seemed like hours of lying there, watching more Union boys than rebel boys drop, the sun dipped behind the trees.

The fighting slowed, then stopped.

Johnny was too scared to move, too scared that if he did, he'd be captured. So he stayed put another hour or so after he heard the last fading voice.

It was pitch-black when he finally stood. He couldn't even see the stars and the moon because the leaves overhead were so thick.

Johnny craned his ear for the sound of the drum.

Only the sound of crickets filled the night.

His heart sped up.

No drum!

No footfalls, no voices.

Nothing but nighttime on a cold, smoky battlefield.

Without the sound of that drum, Johnny was lost.

CHAPTER 17

Johnny slept on the battlefield that night.

But *sleep* was a generous word for it. He wrapped his blanket around himself and shivered, his back against a cold, rough maple tree.

He wasn't afraid of wildlife; the battle had driven away any animals that might've been in this forest.

He was afraid of humans. Any moment now, a rebel could point a musket at his temple or put another sword against his throat.

But he wanted to see a human. Hear a human. Know that he wasn't so lost that he'd starve or freeze to death out here.

Alone.

Johnny couldn't walk through the thick underbrush in this darkness; he tried. He didn't have a lantern (though he couldn't have lit it even if he had it). He'd trip and fall, and then he'd have a wound to deal with out here, too.

No, it was best to stay put.

The moment the air lightened to a purply gray, Johnny leapt out of his blanket and headed north.

He walked for maybe a mile or two in the fog and didn't see a thing.

Except for dead bodies.

He shivered. A lot.

His stomach cramped with hunger; his throat squeezed with thirst.

At last, Johnny came to a place where the trees aligned themselves like rows of orderly soldiers, and he realized he was in an orchard.

He tore peaches and apples off the trees and ate till his belly complained.

And where there was an orchard, there had to be nearby—

"Water!" he yelled out. He couldn't help it. It was a fast-flowing, clear stream. He jumped in it. The cold numbed his skin.

He scooped up a handful of water and brought it to his face, ready to gulp.

And that's when he noticed it.

The water.

It was tinged red.

Upstream, a tangle of bodies lay twisted and bleeding into this stream.

His mouth soured.

Click!

Johnny turned to the sound, and there was a rebel on a horse.

Johnny had left his musket on the banks of the creek so it wouldn't get wet. He was powerless.

There was nothing—*nothing*—Johnny despised more than feeling powerless.

"Surrender, Yank."

Johnny nodded. Raised his hands.

"I surrender."

Some hero I've turned out to be.

———◦◦◦◦———

The rebels tied Johnny's wrists and ankles with rope and marched him south with a group of Union prisoners. If Johnny had thought marching fifteen miles a day was hard, marching fifteen miles a day with rope burns, tied to a hundred other men who tripped and fell and bled and vomited, was horrible.

The prisoners marched for sixteen straight days. At last, they approached a circle of huge wooden walls. It was a prison in Andersonville, Georgia. The moment Johnny was through the gate, he smelled the sickness of the men inside.

The prisoners stopped near the entrance of the prison. A man in a brown uniform (those rebels, with

An illustrated aerial view of Andersonville Prison, including prisoners' tents, gallows, and a stream for washing. Three rows of stockade fences surrounded the prison, and artillery batteries of cannons were stationed at the corners. *[LC-DIG-pga-02585]*

their mismatched clothes!) galloped up and down the line, inspecting his newest Union prisoners.

He drew his horse to a sharp stop in front of Johnny. He hopped down.

"Well, look at this, why don't you!" he narrowed his eyes at Johnny. The cording on the rebel's shoulder told Johnny he was a general. "What do we have here?"

Johnny stuck his chin in the air. "Sergeant John Lincoln Clem of the Twenty-Second Michigan, sir!"

That rebel bent in half, laughing. Johnny seethed.

"Sergeant? Oh! Oh, that's ripe! Come out of that line, boy. Come with me."

"I'd prefer to stay with the other men, sir."

The rebel general slapped his knee and hee-hawed. "Other men!"

He untied Johnny from the Union boys and looped the end of the rope around the horn of his saddle. The general mounted his horse. "Keep up, boy!" he yelled down at Johnny.

Johnny's heart pounded in his chest.

Keep up with a galloping horse after marching for six-teen days?

Luckily, Johnny's ankles were no longer bound, and he ran at a decent clip next to the trotting horse.

"Come 'round, rebels! Come 'round! Get a gander at this!"

Other rebels in brown and gray uniforms gathered while Johnny ran in a circle next to the general's horse. This general wasn't acting very much like a leader. He was no hero in Johnny's eyes.

"Boys, see what sore straits the Yankees are driven to!" the general shouted. "They've sent their babies to fight us!"

Those rebels, they laughed and pointed and screeched that horrible rebel yell, "*IiiiiiEEEEeeeee! IiiiiiEEEEeeee!*"

One of them even took photographs.

Photographs!

So expensive!

So embarrassing!

Finally, after they all had a good long laugh at Johnny, the general stopped and untied him. Johnny fell to his knees, panting.

The rebels drifted away, back to guarding the exhausted Yankees they held prisoner.

Except the guy with the camera. "Son," he said to Johnny, "I'm a newspaper photographer. I work for Mathew Brady. You know Mr. Brady?"

Johnny managed to shake his head.

"Mr. Brady. Remember his name. Because he's going to make you a hero."

Johnny swallowed. "Sir," he croaked despite his dry throat, "my fire has been all but knocked out of me. I'm about sick of this hero business."

CHAPTER 18

Those captors knew how to get the best of Johnny. They took the thing that mattered most in the world to him, his most treasured item.

They took his uniform.

His Union blue jacket.

His Union blue trousers.

His Union blue cap with three holes shot in it.

Johnny cussed the rebels who took those things, all right. They laughed in his face. The newspaper reporter snapped more photos.

Johnny overheard one of the rebels say there were 45,000 Union fellas there in Andersonville. Before the war, Johnny had never even visited the next town over from Newark, Ohio. Now here he was in southern Georgia with the widest variety of people he ever did see: rebel and Union, white and colored, young and old, female and male. So many people. Their stories kept Johnny laughing:

"This bullet wound is gonna make that sweet Mary Caroline fall in love with me the minute I get home."

"Only if that bullet wound can make a diamond ring, too!"

Johnny had to laugh at the stories, because everything else there was downright rotten. The food

Prisoner lean-tos inside Andersonville Prison.
[LC-DIG-highsm-11809]

in the prison camp was abysmal. The rebels ate first, of course, and gave whatever was left to the prisoners. Some of the Union fellas, they hadn't had a fruit or a vegetable in months. Scurvy wracked their bodies, making their hair and teeth fall out. Johnny broke open a hunk of corn bread on the third or fourth day he was there, and it was so moldy, it looked like it had cob-webs in it.

He ate it anyway.

One thing the rebels did do right was take care of the boys who were injured. Doctors fished bullets out of muscle with their fingers. They amputated body parts with sharp saws on rusty, dusty old doors, set up like rows of operating tables. There wasn't much chloroform available to knock the fellas out, so the doctors gave their patients plenty of whiskey.

The arms and legs the doctors removed were tossed into a huge hole, left to rot. The stench and the flies in the camp were downright horrible.

Things were so bad, one of the men two bunks down from Johnny played his flute day and night, with-out stopping, even when the others shouted and threw stones at him. Johnny would sometimes drum his hands on his thighs, playing along with the tunes he

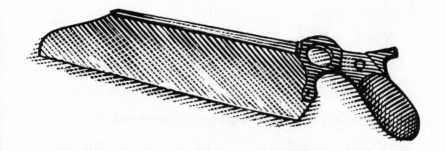

knew. The old guy would smile his toothless smile and keep playing with wet eyes.

About a week after Johnny arrived, while he was drumming along with Toothless Joe, someone walked up behind him.

"Johnny Shiloh."

Johnny turned. Because the sun was behind this fella, he couldn't see his face. But his arm was busted apart and hung limply in a bloody sling.

Johnny stood.

"William!"

Now Johnny could see: William's arm wasn't just busted—it had been removed at the elbow. William caught Johnny staring.

"No more drumming for me," William said, waving his arm and wincing. "Which means no paycheck. I'm gonna be useless on the farm, too."

His voice was strong while he said these things, firm but hollow.

"Gosh, William. I'm sorry."

William shrugged his bony shoulders. Johnny realized then how skinny he was. How dirty. How sick.

"How long have you been here?" he asked.

William smiled, and Johnny saw he was missing some of his teeth, too. "Can't quite recall."

"Are there others from the Third Ohio here?"

"There are."

In a matter of minutes, Johnny was reunited with Captain McDougal and a few others from the Third. They hugged and smacked one another on the back. They all looked as dirty and sick as William.

Johnny and the others swapped stories for a bit, the fellas all laughing when Johnny reenacted capturing that Southern colonel by hiding under a fake cannon.

"Sounds like the Johnny Shiloh I know," William said.

Just then, a rebel came over to them. "You," he said, lifting his chin at Johnny. "You're John Lincoln Clem?"

"I am."

"Come with me," the rebel said. "General Wheeler wants a word with you."

———◦◦◦◦———

"The *New York Herald*," General Wheeler said when Johnny entered the barrack. The general flung a thick newspaper down on his table. "The *Charleston Mercury*." He tossed another newspaper on top of it. "Even *Harper's Weekly*, for crying out loud!"

Johnny narrowed his eyes at General Wheeler. This was the same general who'd tied Johnny to his horse and trotted him around the prison camp the day he arrived. "Sir?"

"Look!" the general bellowed, and jammed his thumb on the top newspaper. There, on the front page, was Johnny's picture!

Child Hero Captured by Confederates read the head-line.

Johnny beamed: *Hero!*

But still: *Child.*

He shrugged. "Looks like that Mathew Brady fella got the story he wanted."

General Wheeler growled and threw the newspaper

at the opposite wall. "Every eyeball in the country is on you now, kid. I can't let you get hurt, you understand? You get sick or killed, and it's my hide!"

Johnny tried not to smile.

General Wheeler got up, paced the room. "I can't have the reputation for hurting kids, see. That won't do. That won't do for my career."

"You shoulda thought about that before you tied me to your horse, sir."

The general spun about on his heel. "No lip, kid. I'm not known for my patience, understand?"

Johnny swallowed. "Yes, sir."

General Wheeler ran the palm of his hand over his face, pulling the loose skin taut. "You, uh . . ." He paused, and it seemed to pain him to say the rest. "You need anything while you're here, kid?"

Johnny's pride almost had him shout, *I don't need a stinking thing from you, you lousy traitor!*

But luckily, Johnny's brain was bigger than his pride.

"Yes, sir," he said, bouncing on his toes. "I need a crate of peaches. No, make that two. And a pair of size twelve boots."

CHAPTER 19

The other Union fellas ate those peaches like they were made of gold, which they kind of were. The juice dribbled over their fingers and down their chins, cleaning away little rivers of dust and dirt. They cried. Those fellas cried when they ate that fruit.

The new boots fit William perfectly, too, though he fought Johnny like a bobcat before he accepted them.

Over the next month, Johnny bartered with the rebels for everything he could: corn, apples, pumpkins, clothes, playing cards, writing paper, lye soap, extra water, a drum.

A photograph of John Lincoln Clem in uniform in 1863.
[Wikimedia Commons, Treadwell & Peaslee]

All because he was this famous kid. His celebrity bought those things.

The Butternuts (which the Union boys had taken to calling the rebels, because those who wore brown uniforms had dyed the cloth by boiling it with butternuts) eased up on their prisoners a little, and some nights, they even played music together: Johnny on drums, Toothless Joe on flute, and some of those Butternut guards on the fife and bugle.

"We make nice music together," one of those rebel fellas said to Johnny after a loud, swaying round of "Home, Sweet Home!"

He smiled. "That we do."

Sometimes Johnny thought that if it were up to him and that particular group of rebels, they'd have that war over and done with in a half hour's time.

The Union fellas grew stronger with the fruits and vegetables Johnny gave them.

For the first time since he stowed away in that train car when he was nine years old, he made a real difference.

He felt like a true hero.

And it was all because he was this famous kid. It wouldn't have happened otherwise, he knew. Johnny wouldn't be famous if he wasn't still a kid.

Because Johnny was a kid, he was able to be a hero.

———◦◦◦◦———

Johnny had been in Andersonville about eight weeks when General Wheeler sent for him again late one evening. The general barely looked up from his desk, and his face was hidden in shadows. "Kid, you're getting out."

"What?" Johnny couldn't hide the snappiness in his voice. "No, sir, I—"

General Wheeler looked up at last. He smirked at Johnny. "You'd rather stay in prison."

Johnny took a deep breath. "I believe I'm needed here, sir."

General Wheeler flashed a fancy stamped letter.

"Well, the Union thinks otherwise. You, specifically, have been selected for a prisoner exchange."

Johnny shook his head. "Sir, is there any way—"

"Look, kid," General Wheeler said. He looked tired in the jumpy glow of the lantern light. "You'll be free. And we're getting twenty Confederate soldiers in exchange for you. Twenty, just for you.

"And honestly," he continued, "I can't afford to keep you. Peaches and apples and corn? You're breaking me, kid."

Johnny grinned.

Surprisingly, General Wheeler did, too.

"Though I have to admit," he said in a near whisper. "My boys have liked the extra fruits and vegetables, too."

The general signed the piece of paper and handed it to Johnny.

Then the Confederate general stood.

And he saluted Johnny.

Johnny saluted him back.

"You're a good soldier, you know that, kid?"

"Yes, sir," Johnny replied. "I do."

"I don't want to leave," Johnny told William and the others.

"You're crazy," William said. "The war has officially made you nuts."

But he smiled.

And he pointed his healing half arm at Johnny. "You go. And you keep that new uniform clean, you hear?"

Johnny looked down at his new duds. A couple of sweet old ladies in Chicago read in one of the newspapers how devastated he was when the rebels took his uniform. So they made him a new one and shipped it to the prison for his release. It fit perfectly, and it was clean. No holes, no dirt, no blood.

Johnny yanked the hem of his jacket. "I will. At least until the lice get me."

They laughed, and Johnny thought it was a good time to swing his leg up and over the horse that was carrying him out of there.

"Good-bye, fellas," Johnny shouted down to them. "Union glory!"

"Union glory!" they shouted back, and the Butternuts laughed because who but a bunch of stubborn fools would shout that while in prison!

And—oh.

A horse!

Johnny hadn't been on a horse since he left home. He'd forgotten how it felt to have the wind in his hair and the muscular power galloping beneath him.

They covered so much ground, so quickly, Johnny riding behind a rebel in the saddle. They headed north for the exchange.

They'd been galloping about an hour when they slowed to look for water.

Suddenly: a crack, a whistle, another and another.

The horse below Johnny collapsed.

The rebel in front of him did, too.

White-hot pain blazed across the tip of Johnny's ear and through his hip.

He was shot.

CHAPTER 20

Johnny lay there for what felt like days, but was probably only minutes. Pain throbbed through him with every pulse of his heart, drumming as fast as stroking ruffles on a snare.

"Hold your fire!" he heard someone yell. "That's a Union soldier!"

Johnny's vision blacked out. When the circle of light behind his eyes grew wide again, two Union blue fellas hovered overhead.

"That's not just any soldier," one of them said. "It's a kid!"

The other fella shook his head. "That's not just any kid. That's Johnny Shiloh!"

Johnny hardly recalled getting loaded into their wagon and dragged to the hospital. The doctor there placed a rag over his face that smelled strong, but slightly sweet. Chloroform. That stuff knocked him out good.

When he woke the next day, his head was spinning and pounding, and his ear and hip stung like the devil himself had reached up and sizzled them.

"You're all patched up," a nice nurse said. She looked like an angel, standing over him in her long dress and small pointy hat. "You took a shell fragment to your hip and lost the tip of your left ear."

Johnny reached up to his ear, but it was bandaged.

"Nice!" he said.

She laughed. "I bet your mother is real proud of you, honey."

Instead of Johnny's heart squeezing with pain at the word *mother*, it squeezed with pride. "I think she is."

"You need to head home for a couple of months to heal, though. That hip of yours needs rest."

"Home?" Johnny asked. "Lebanon?" He sure did miss Tennessee.

"No."

"Covington?" Kentucky! He hadn't been back there in almost two years!

"No, Johnny," the nurse said. She smiled. "Home. Newark, Ohio."

Oh.

Home.

Johnny stood on the train platform, waiting. Wind whooshed all around, stirring up dust and leaflets of paper. The engine chuffed past, the wheels squealing to a stop.

The roar of train wheels was nothing compared to the roar of a battlefield.

Johnny's drum was louder than those wheels, he reckoned. If his drum could be heard over a battle, it could be heard over these wheels.

He and his drum were more powerful than train wheels.

He was so tired. He limped aboard the train car and placed his head against the window's cool glass.

Soon enough, the train rolled out of the station.

He wasn't sweating and shaking underneath the seat as a stowaway. He wasn't counting to thirteen.

The train rocked from side to side as it moved down the track.

Johnny fell asleep, dreaming of drumbeats and angels.

———◦◦◦◦———

"Johnny," the train conductor said, shaking his shoulder. "This is your stop, son."

Johnny rubbed the sleep from his eyes. He stood, stretched, and made his way off the train.

"Johnny!"

Lizzie and Louis tackled him, and he didn't once complain about the pain that shot through his hip. His eyes stung with tears.

"Look at the two of you!" he said. "Louis, you're taller than me!"

Louis had a good inch on him. His little brother smiled. "I figured I'd beat you."

"And, Lizzie! Let me look at you! You're such a young lady. You look just like"—Johnny paused and swallowed—"Mama. You really do."

Lizzie bounced on her toes. "Everybody says so."

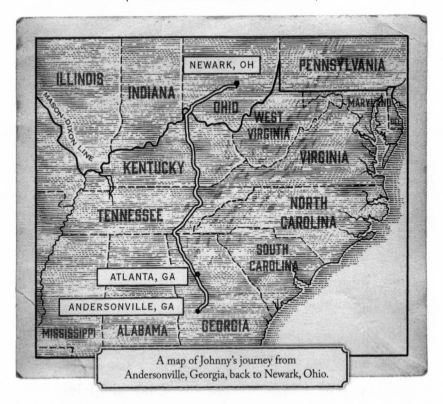

A map of Johnny's journey from
Andersonville, Georgia, back to Newark, Ohio.

"John Joseph."

Johnny looked over his siblings' shoulders to his pop. Tears streamed down his father's face. Pop clutched newspaper clippings. When Johnny looked closer, he saw they were all about him.

"We thought you were dead, John Joseph. That day at the church, you told Liz and Lou you were going swimming. We dredged the canal and everything. Years we thought you were dead. Then we see these." Pop lifted the clippings.

Holy cow.

They thought Johnny had *drowned*!

Guilt flooded through him like a sickness. Pop probably hated him! And Johnny wouldn't blame him one bit. What he'd done back then, it was as cowardly and dishonest as Harry streaking away from the battle back in Shiloh. "Pop, I—"

Pop lunged forward and smothered Johnny in a hug. "I'm so happy you're alive, John Joseph." He wept into Johnny's hair. He smelled like soap and pine needles.

That hug, those tears.

That was what forgiveness felt like.

Pop pulled back, placed his hands on Johnny's shoulders, and looked him in the eye.

"You're a hero, John Joseph."

Johnny smiled. "John Lincoln."

Pop nodded once and smiled, too. "John Lincoln."

———◦◦◦———

On the other side of the train station, a huge crowd had gathered. Everyone Johnny knew in all of Newark was there, it seemed. They cheered and clapped and waved flags when he stepped through the station doors.

A brass band kicked up, and there beneath all the hurrahs and hubbub, he heard it:

The drum.

Johnny's heart thrummed along with the tune they played:

When Johnny comes marching home again,
Hurrah! Hurrah!
We'll give him a hearty welcome then,
Hurrah! Hurrah!
The men will cheer and the boys will shout,
The ladies, they will all turn out,
And we'll all feel gay,
When Johnny comes marching home.

The old church bell will peal with joy,
Hurrah! Hurrah!
To welcome home our darling boy,
Hurrah! Hurrah!
The village lads and lassies say
With roses they will strew the way,
And we'll all feel gay,
When Johnny comes marching home.

EPILOGUE

After his hip healed, Johnny went back into battle. He fought at Resaca and Kennesaw before the war ended in April 1865. He would've just stuck around, but one of his superiors pointed north and said, "Get back to school, Johnny. The best soldiers know much more than war."

A year after the war ended, Johnny was still sleeping on the floor at Pop's house. He just couldn't get comfortable in a bed. Too soft. All those years sleeping on the ground spoiled him.

This particular morning, Johnny rose from his pallet on the floor when there was a knock at the door.

He swung the heavy door wide. On the front stoop

stood a young fella, maybe twelve years old. He was a freed slave—Johnny knew from the brand seared into the flesh on his arm.

The fella held up a newspaper clipping. "You're John Lincoln Clem?"

Johnny winced, only because he hated seeing that photo of him from so long ago, dirty and tied to that horse. He wished the photo was of him looking dapper in his uniform. "I am."

The young fella extended his hand. Johnny shook it. It was rough from years of hard work. "Name's Elijah. I'm Jackson's brother."

Johnny's face nearly split in two with his smile. "No joshing? Come in, come in! Have a seat! Where's your—"

He realized, though, before he finished the sentence, that if Jackson wasn't here, too, the news wasn't good.

Elijah entered but didn't sit. "Jackson died at the Battle of Poison Spring. One of his regiment found me after the war and told me."

"You—" Johnny's voice broke off. He had a hard time finding it to finish: "He didn't find you before he died?"

"No."

Johnny dropped into a nearby chair.

The Union had won.

But winning came with so much losing.

Elijah shifted and held out a parcel wrapped in brown paper. "The man from his regiment gave this to me. Jackson told him that I had to find you and give it to you."

Johnny unwrapped the parcel.

There, inside, were his two rosewood drumsticks.

They were still shiny and heavy. Jackson had taken excellent care of them.

A small piece of paper was wrapped around them:

John Lincoln, it read. *You saved my life. Here are the sticks I borrowed. Forever thanks, Jackson.*

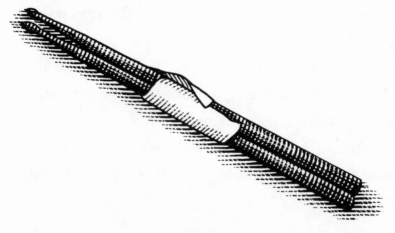

On the flip side of the paper? The number *18*.

Sometimes, you don't know whether to laugh or cry, so you do both.

Elijah stayed for supper. Then throughout the night, Johnny and Elijah swapped stories and sang songs and laughed. And cried.

Yes, a soldier cries sometimes.

When Elijah readied himself to leave, Johnny's heart sped. He realized how young twelve years old looked, now that he was fifteen. "Where are you going? Won't you stay?"

Elijah shook his head. "No, I need to go find work, you know . . ." He smiled. "I'm a free man now."

AUTHOR'S NOTE

*"The United States don't need the service
of boys who disobey their parents."*

—PRESIDENT ABRAHAM LINCOLN

John Lincoln Clem was born John Joseph Klem in Newark, Ohio, on August 13, 1851. When he was nine, his mother was killed by a train. Later that same year, he became so enamored with the idea of restoring the divided Union that he volunteered his services to Captain Leonidas McDougal of the Third Ohio Union Regiment, thinking, he said years later, "my help was obviously needed." And according to Johnny, Captain McDougal did indeed laugh and retort, "I'm not enlisting infants, son."

It was not the custom for boys as young as nine to join the army, but in the Civil War, boys age fourteen, fifteen, or sixteen weren't uncommon. A boy oftentimes joined alongside his father or grandfather, and the army accepted him as a full enlisted soldier as long as his parents okayed it. But Johnny's father refused.

And so, as in the story, Johnny told his brother, Louis, and his sister, Lizzie, that he was skipping church to swim in the canal. But instead of swimming, nine-year-old Johnny stowed away on a train.

In truth, it is believed that Johnny was discovered quite quickly and was placed on the next train home. His father, in the meantime, believed Johnny had drowned. He had dredged the canal, looking for Johnny's body. Needless to say, Johnny was in a heap of trouble after that. But Johnny couldn't resist the call to aid the Union. Again, on May 24, 1861, the nine-year-old ran away and hid on an outgoing train carrying the Third Ohio volunteer regiment. And this second time, the boy made it all the way to Covington, Kentucky, where his army adventures began. He was quickly adopted as a "mascot," was paid thirteen dollars a month by the other soldiers in his regiment, and was given a uniform and a drum.

Where Johnny went next and who he went with is a bit of a mystery. (Since he wasn't officially enlisted, the records aren't exactly accurate.) Some historians say there is no way John Clem (who adopted the middle name "Lincoln" upon joining the army and changed the spelling of his last name along the way) could've been a drummer boy at the Battle of Shiloh. Their argument: The Twenty-Second Michigan, which ultimately enlisted Johnny, hadn't even mustered yet (they gathered in Pontiac, Michigan, on August 29, 1862).

But there are about fifteen months between when Johnny ran away from home and when the Twenty-Second Michigan became a regiment and headed south. The Battle of Shiloh took place during that time, on April 6 and 7, 1862. John Clem himself claims he was at Shiloh. He likely could've been there with another regiment, and it appears that some members of the Third Ohio, Johnny's home regiment, did indeed fight at Shiloh. So, for the sake of the story and to honor John Clem's personal account of the battle, the author assumes that Johnny began the Civil War with the Third Ohio, then later enlisted with the Twenty-Second Michigan.

At Shiloh, Johnny was ordered by General Ulysses S. Grant to play the Long Roll—the Advance—without stopping. It was an aggressive tactic on General Grant's part. According to several accounts, General Grant praised Johnny's bravery as his drummer during the bloody battle that took place on the Mississippi-Tennessee border. Clem says of the Battle of Shiloh, "At Shiloh, my drum was smashed by a fragment of shell. They called me 'Johnny Shiloh' for a while after that."

At the age of twelve, John Clem also fought at the

Battle of Chickamauga (September 19–20, 1863) with a sawed-off musket. He was made a sergeant prior to the battle. (Though, according to Clem, it was General George Henry Thomas who officially enlisted him in this way, not Rosecrans as in the story. Clem admits to being disappointed with the position, saying, "General, is that all you're going to make me?") When asked why he traded the drum for a rifle, John Clem said, "because I did not like to stand and be shot at without shooting back."

Johnny's hat showed his service in the battle, thanks to three clean bullet holes it gained. And Clem did, in fact, injure a Confederate colonel at Chickamauga, after the colonel demanded that *he* surrender. (Clem later wrote of the incident, "I am glad to be able to add that, according to advices afterwards received, the Confederate colonel recovered from his wound.")

And Clem did ultimately survive the Battle of Chickamauga by playing possum. "I decided that the best policy was to fall dead for the moment, and so I did," Clem later wrote. "I lay dead until after dark, when I 'came alive' again and managed to find my way to Chattanooga."

John Clem was captured after the Battle of Chickamauga, though he likely wasn't imprisoned at Andersonville. That location was chosen for this story for its uniqueness—it was so large, and because it's now a historic site, ample information about it is available.

Says Clem: "A few days after the battle of Chickamauga I was captured, and was held a prisoner for two months before being exchanged. It was at this period that I was exhibited by [Confederate] General 'Joe' Wheeler as the fighting Yankee 'baby.'

"My captors had no sympathetic interest in Yankee babies in uniform," Clem added. "They stole my jacket; they stole my shoes; they even stole my cap, which I was most anxious to preserve, on account of the bullet holes. I wish I had it now."

The newspapers went wild with accounts of the little hero drummer boy, Johnny Shiloh, imprisoned by the rebels. "It was this incident," Clem wrote later, "a report of which was spread through the newspapers, that inspired the Chicago ladies . . . with the idea of providing a fine uniform for little Johnny Clem." It's not certain if one of Mathew Brady's team members took the photo that made Clem famous. Brady was (and still is) known for his photography of the Civil War. He had a team of photographers who worked for him, so it's possible that the photographer who took Clem's photograph worked for Brady. Clem was, later in his career, photographed by Brady himself.

Clem did receive two injuries in the war (though when, exactly, is unclear). "I was wounded only twice," he said. "Once when a piece of shell struck me in the hip, and the other time, at Atlanta, when . . . a ball nipped my ear. On the later occasion my pony was killed under me. These were mere scratches."

And finally, the story of Johnny shooting the local farmer's pig is true, and one that John Clem told several times later in his life. He supposedly did tell the Union General Doolittle, "You wouldn't let a rebel pig bite *you*, would you?" And the Union troops feasted on pig that evening, thanks to Johnny.

Other details in this story are true for Civil War soldiers as a whole, but maybe didn't happen to John Clem directly: getting punched in the chest for the "medical exam," having a dog as a mascot, giving the winter quarters names like "Buzzard's Roost," making bullets over the fire, playing cards and gambling for brass buttons, walking twenty-two miles on a "good" day, raiding farms for food, racing lice on a tin plate, eating little more than hardtack for days, getting dysentery, writing your name on a slip of paper before heading into battle, using hot-air balloons in combat, being fooled by Quaker guns, surviving the prison conditions. *All* of these happened to soldiers in the Civil War, but whether or not they each happened to John Clem isn't certain.

The chores that Johnny performs in the story— drumming calls, giving haircuts, fetching water, keeping camp clean, searching battlefields for wounded soldiers— were all typical of a Civil War drummer boy.

Also, unfortunately, the gruesome descriptions of the battle scenes were adapted from letters that soldiers wrote home to their loved ones. They are accurate, but less horrific than the actual descriptions from the soldiers themselves.

A few of the characters in the story—Harry, William, and Elijah, namely—are fictional. Jackson, however, was a real drummer boy. It's unlikely that he and John Clem knew each other, but the character in the story is based on an escaped slave who drummed for the Seventy-Ninth Colored. Jackson's last name appears to be unknown.

Jackson, a runaway slave who was discovered in tattered clothing, joined the Seventy-Ninth Colored volunteer regiment in Louisiana. Photographs of him in tattered clothing, paired with photographs of him in his Union uniform and drum, were circulated to encourage enlistments among African Americans during the war. In the story, Jackson dies in the Battle of Poison Spring, where the Seventy-Ninth Colored was known to have fought. However, very little is known about Jackson's actual service and what became of him after the war. Many African Americans fought in the Civil War. Approximately 10 percent of the Union troops were black (about 179,000 soldiers). About 19,000 African Americans served in the navy. By the time the Civil War ended, almost 40,000 black soldiers had died.

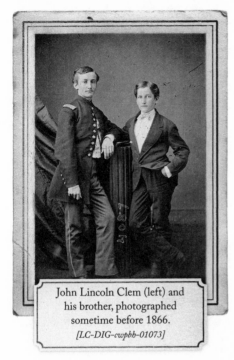

John Lincoln Clem (left) and his brother, photographed sometime before 1866.
[LC-DIG-cwpbh-01073]

After the Civil War, John Clem was honorably mustered out of service at the age of thirteen. He returned home for more schooling, and later tried to enter West Point. "But alas . . . schooling, rather than military experience, was the prime requisite [to enter the military academy]," he wrote. "I had left school to go to war before I was ten years old, and my scholarship was sadly in arrears.

"That was certainly hard luck," Clem continued. "What is the use of being a Civil War veteran, bearing honorable scars, if in one's old age—the age of twenty, let us say, in [hind]sight—one is turned down by an unappreciative Government?"

So Clem went to see an old buddy: General Ulysses S. Grant, who just so happened to be president by this time. Grant said, "We can do better than that," and appointed Clem second lieutenant. Clem studied further at Fort Monroe.

John Clem married the daughter of a Confederate veteran and had three children. He retired from the army as a major general in 1916 and was the oldest active Civil War veteran. John died in 1937 when he was eighty-five years old. He is buried at Arlington National Cemetery.

A six-foot-tall statue of young Johnny Clem stands near the Buckingham Meeting House in Newark, Ohio. A World War II transport and hospital ship was named *John L. Clem* in his honor. A public school in Ohio is named John Clem Elementary after him, and in 1963, Walt Disney produced a made-for-TV movie called *Johnny Shiloh* that detailed Clem's life.

"War is bald, naked savagery," Clem wrote late in his life. "As compared with the adult man, the boy is near to the savage.

"Boys make first-rate soldiers," he continued. "To begin with, they have in highest degree what the French call *élan,* a word feebly translated as 'dash.' They are, above all, ambitious to do things, and in them the spirit of caution is not yet developed."

John Clem led an extraordinary life, shaped by the choice he made at nine years old when he stowed away on a train.

GLOSSARY

OF TERMS

artillery: The troops that specialize in firing large weapons, like cannons.

barrel shirt: A punishment in which a soldier was forced to wear a barrel as a shirt. Three holes were cut in a barrel: one for a head, two for arms. Soldiers completed their drills in it, marching while carrying the massive extra weight of a barrel.

barter: To trade items rather than use money.

canal: A man-made waterway.

cavalry: The part of a military force that serves on horseback.

civilian: A person who is not on active duty with the military.

confederate/confederacy: A group united in alliance;

the Southern states that seceded from the Union declared themselves "the Confederate States of America," or the "Confederacy."

dishonorable: A "discharge" is given when a member of the military is released from his/her service. To be "dishonorably discharged" means that the person did not fulfill the obligations of his/her service before release.

economy: The management of a region's or country's resources.

enlist: To enroll voluntarily for military service.

fire-eaters: A nickname for Southerners who were passionate about secession.

grape, the: A type of cannon fire. It was called this because it was actually hundreds of bits of lead, rather than one large ball, and so it looked like bunches of grapes.

hardtack: A simple type of cracker made from flour, water, and salt. Also jokingly called "tooth dullers" or "worm castles."

in bivouac: A temporary soldier encampment, which may include sleeping on the ground (rather than on a pallet).

infantry: Soldiers who fight on foot.

minié ball: A cone-shaped soft lead bullet. Its name comes from its inventor, Claude-Étienne Minié.

musket: A light gun with a long barrel used by the infantry. It was typically fired from the shoulder.

muster: To gather or assemble; when troops *muster*, it is for battle, display, inspection, orders, discharge, or to undertake some other activity as a group.

Napoleons: The nickname for the Union's heavy iron cannons.

one cat and two cats: A game close to baseball. The troops played many pickup games like these while camped.

orderly drummer: The head drummer. This was usually rotated day to day or week to week. The orderly drummer was "on call," meaning that person was *the* drummer whenever one was needed during that period.

orders: Commands issued to troops.

pillage: To steal with violence or without regard for others.

platform: The area alongside train tracks. The cars of the train are entered from the *platform*.

Quaker guns: Fake cannons made from wood, fence posts, and wagon wheels. These were used to make it appear that an army was much more powerful than it actually was.

rashers: Fatty salt pork; bacon.

rebel: A person who refuses allegiance to a government

or ruler. This was a common nickname for Southern troops and citizens by those living in Northern states.

regiment: Ground forces comprised of two or more fighting units. They were numbered and labeled by the state where they mustered: the Third Ohio, the Twenty-Second Michigan.

salt horse: Meat preserved with salt; bacon could be considered "salt horse."

secede: To leave or split away from something.

slave collar: An iron collar placed on slaves who were considered a risk of escaping. It had long arms with bells on them so runaway slaves could be heard.

states' rights: The rights and powers held by the individual states, rather than by the federal government.

tariffs: Fees charged by a government on imports and exports.

wheel/wheeling: A military maneuver used to change direction of troops. In it, one end of the line of soldiers remains stationary while the other end of the line turns, or "wheels" around to face a new direction.

Yankee: The nickname used for Northerners, people north of the Mason-Dixon line.

GLOSSARY

OF DRUM CALLS

Advance: Also called the *Alarm* or the *Long Roll*. A call to arms on the battlefield, or used in emergencies. It was usually drummed by advanced drummers, and it was considered an honor to play.

Assemble/Assembly: In camp, this drum call signaled the troops to gather. In battle, it called the soldiers to a certain area (not an emergency).

Breakfast Call: The beat that called the troops to breakfast. This varied from regiment to regiment, but was often the popular tune "Peas Upon a Trencher."

Cease-Fire: A battle call to stop firing weapons.

Church Call: Played to gather troops for church services or when a truce was reached.

Commence Fire: A battle call to begin firing weapons.

Direct Step Call: A marching drumbeat, this was the most common pace for marching soldiers. Because many men marched in a single regiment, drumbeats were used to communicate to the entire length of the line.

Drummer's Call: A beat used to gather the drummers and musicians.

General: The "break camp" call, which meant soldiers should pack up their belongings because it was time to move out.

Halt: A marching call that meant "stop."

Left Wheel: The left wheel, the right wheel, and all other troop movements had their own drumbeats, in order to direct the troops to where they were needed in battle.

Long Roll: Also called the *Advance* or *Alarm*. See *Advance* above.

Officer's Call: A call to gather the officers.

Pioneer's Call: A "clean the camp" call, this beat was drummed when it was time to clean trash and manure out of the campsite. This call was also used mean-spiritedly when troops drove a scoundrel out of camp.

Quickstep: A marching call, a pace faster than a Direct Step (see above).

Retreat: In camp, this marked the end of the workday, so it was a very welcome call. In battle, this call meant to reverse the attack, head back to the starting point, and give up any ground covered or gained. When the retreat sounded in battle, soldiers would fire one last time if their guns were loaded before heading backward.

Reveille: Soldiers were expected to wake, dress, and report to roll call by the time reveille was done.

Salute: This call was played when a high-ranking official entered the camp.

Surgeon's Call: Directed soldiers to medical aid.

Taps: A lights-out call at day's end. This is still symbolically played at funerals.

Water Call: A signal to the troops to gather water.

Wood Call: A signal to the troops to gather wood.

ML 2/2016